Bigger & Badder

JACKSON KANE

HOT TREE PUBLISHING

For information, contact the publisher, Hot Tree Publishing.

www.hottreepublishing.com

Editing: Hot Tree Editing

Cover Designer: BookSmith Design

E-book ISBN: 978-1-922359-27-8

Paperback ISBN: 978-1-922359-28-5

Dedicated to Tasha Hooks and to Harlow Kane. Without their patience, support, guidance and friendship this book wouldn't exist. Thank you for everything, ladies.

ONE

GARRETT

"We're entering Caldwell Hope now, sir." Mitch's voice squawked over my luxury helicopter's intercom. I'd have flown myself, but I used the travel time to make a few conference calls.

My thumbs rotated their respective black bands as I watched the mountaintops fall away to reveal the smattering of lights of the valley below. They looked like a ball of old Christmas lights that no one bothered to untangle before they plugged them in. *Fitting, what with the end of the year holidays only a few weeks away and all.*

"I shouldn't be back here," I spoke the words quietly to myself, idly fingering the black tungsten ring I wore on each hand's ring finger. Immediately a wave of unease sank into my stomach like I'd swallowed hot lead paste.

From this height, I could see how empty the town

had become. An early Wednesday night in a resort town during their busy season should've been bristling with activity. It wasn't. Even some of the shops on the main strip had darkened windows.

That bunch of Christmas lights had far too many blown bulbs.

My watch face lit up with a deposit notification. My birthday goal was so close I could taste it. I scrolled to the next email. It was a forwarded message from my assistant, Michael. My nomination into the Pro Football Hall of Fame had been approved.

Not bad. I was going to be the youngest person to ever hit thirty billion and one of next year's hall-of-famers. It felt good, in the way eating a pint of ice cream in one sitting does. The feeling was too fleeting.

I should've been on top of the world, but I couldn't shake a feeling that this was a mistake. Caldwell Hope had been the beginning of the end for Heidi and me.

That was a long time ago. I have to let it go.

The pilot banked right. The white and yellow dots of street and shop lights gave way to a blazing torch. The CW Kings Stadium came into view, in all of its grand, hopeful, and stupidly *unfinished* glory.

"Touch down in three minutes, sir."

I told Mitch to swing around. I wanted to see what they were trying to hide. In the wide arc I saw the rest of the city. I'd read the dossier and compared it in my mind against the last time I'd come to town so long ago now. It was more of an idyllic, tourist *village* than a city, especially now that the coal industry had completely dried up.

High above the valley, a palatial mansion was nestled into a gloomy mountain face; it overlooked the small wounded kingdom that was Caldwell Hope. Massive amounts of light radiated off the mansion, staving off the choking darkness. It was a comforting nightlight for an entire town.

Don't worry, it seemed to say, *everything's going to be all right.*

I knew better.

They didn't invite the Grim Reaper of Wall Street into their town if they had any other options.

A large swath of flat blackness on the valley floor was broken by pin pricks of flood lighting. The golf course? I jerked forward and leaned over in my seat and spotted the clubhouse. Immediately, I thought of dancing with the girl I'd *almost* met that Halloween night.

Funny... all these years later and I'd never fully stopped thinking about her.

My pilot began his descent into the parking lot, which was the previously agreed on landing zone. The front entrance of the stadium was awash with color and music for my arrival. There were city officials, news vans, and a full band. This felt more like a rock concert than a business meeting.

I'd been to red carpet functions with less pomp.

I sighed, checking my watch. Four hours until my last and most important appointment of the night. Plenty of time.

This wasn't what we agreed on. I told them to keep this small and out of the news. Was this their way of forcing me to help? Expose me to the press and have public opinion lean on me?

"Hey, Mitch? How many cameras you think they have on us?"

They didn't know who they were dealing with if they thought they could *shame* me into saving their town.

"No idea, sir"

"What do you say we give them a show?" I opened a small compartment overhead and unzipped the bag inside. Glancing back out the window, I could see dozens of people huddled together under massive exterior heat lamps to keep from freezing in the bitter December wind. *Well, they were about to warm up.* "Pull back up and take me over the twenty-yard line. I'm going to take the express way down."

TWO

JUDY

"This is ridiculous!" my dad shouted. "Where the hell is he going?"

"Paul...." A board member groped for my dad distractedly while following our guest's flight with his eyes, then tapped his shoulder when we all noticed the helicopter stop and hover high above the stadium.

The helicopter was a dark blot before a cloudless moon. The gesture was chilling and grand; it felt like we were all being surveyed by an alien or *a god*.

There were nearly fifteen of us crowded together beneath the heat lamps of the main stadium entrance: my father, five other board members, Monica, who was the head of Public Relations, a three-piece string band, several assistants, and me. That wasn't counting the associated press and the government officials.

What the hell was *I* doing here?

My dad slapped the board member's hand away. Dad was the board's chairman and demanded respect from his contemporaries. He was about to reprimand the man when my gasp startled us.

My hands cupped my mouth and I screamed as I watched a speck break off that dark blot and come plummeting toward the ground. I couldn't form sentences if my life depended on it, but if I could've, I would've screamed, *Holy fucking shit, someone just fell out of the helicopter!*

My dad grabbed me as if somehow he could protect me from the chaos of the world. My stomach clenched, then lurched. I just knew that hearing the impact was going to make me sick. Watching whoever it was fall terrified me, but not for my own safety.

I'd never seen anyone die before....

Then a parachute opened.

"Oh, thank God!" I sighed, feeling like I was about to fall over from relief. I was suddenly freezing. The excitement had made me sweat, which made the cold winter air chill me to the bone.

A wave of disapproval made its way through the crowd on the ground. They obviously weren't pleased by our guest's showy entrance, but they kept their voices down, not wanting a man hundreds of feet above us to hear them. As if that were even possible.

Were they that scared of this guy?

I watched the falling man's form slowly descend, becoming more and more man-shaped by the second. "Who is this guy?"

"Garrett Walker," Monica answered curtly, as if the name should mean something to me. All I knew about him was that he was some rich investor. I wasn't asked to do any research. I was just told to be here by Dad for my never-ending quest of "getting experience."

"The Grim Reaper of Wall Street," Monica said, shooting a glare at me that spoke volumes about me not belonging here.

Monica didn't like me, but she was careful not to show it too much. I was, after all, the boss's daughter. That made me the most popular outcast no matter how friendly I was or how hard I worked.

In this case she was right, though. I had no business meeting some pompous billionaire. It was a different story back when I co-owned Black Rocket Records, but... that was another life.

"So... are we glossing over the fact that our potential investor just jumped out of a friggin' helicopter?" The words tumbled out of my mouth as I looked around for confirmation that his actions were the craziest thing to ever happen. "Everyone saw that, right?"

I knew we desperately needed money, but how could

we be okay with this? Obviously this person was out of their mind. Who did something like that?

"His father warned me that Garrett was a little on the unorthodox side." Dad's mouth gaped in awe as he watched the man's descent.

"Unorthodox is wearing a teal suit with an orange cowboy hat, Dad. This guy is downright insane! Do you really want to partner up with someone who thinks gravity is a viable mode of transportation?"

"Attend and observe, daughter," he repeated from earlier in the day. Then he gave me a look that said, *and try not to talk too much.*

That wasn't my fault. I always talked a lot when I got nervous. And knowing how much was riding on this meeting... I was plenty nervous.

All I wanted to do was go home, listen to some music, and paint.

"Also, don't mention Aaron Miller around Garrett," Dad warned. "Those two have the biggest rivalry in sports history."

I thought about asking for clarification, but I decided to wait until after the meeting for that. I doubted I'd even be able to remember that Aaron guy's name, let alone use it, while Garrett was around.

We all stood in front of a one-hundred-fifty-foot wall of shining metal and glass. The main entrance was by far the most finished and presentable part of the stadium—

that's why we were all set up there. I might not have known who this billionaire was, but I did know how meticulously the meeting was planned.

Garrett Walker was supposed to be greeted here with music and smiles, then be ushered into the luxury boxes for hors d'oeuvres and buttery small talk. He'd be given displays and presentations, then be taken through a carefully laid out "guided" tour that showed off the best of what the Caldwell Hope stadium had to offer.

Apparently Garrett had other ideas.

"Sonofabitch," Dad cursed, pushing past several people still dazed by the presentation. "He's headed into the field. Let's go. Move your asses, people! Christ, it's like I'm dealing with that damn King boy."

Now there was a mad dash to preserve as much of that first impression as possible. The band abruptly stopped playing; one musician even dropped their instrument when they were shoved accidentally by a rushing board member. Everyone frantically dashed through Gate A past the ticket lines, through the unfinished seating sections, and out to the field itself.

I was struggling to keep up with the pack. I wore a white dress that was warm but restrictive as hell. My only saving grace was that I wore flats and not heels. I was already taller than my boss and didn't want to give Monica any more reasons to hate me.

Garrett Walker stood alone at the forty-yard line and

tugged at the cuff of his suit jacket, straightening it. He looked like James Bond standing there unfazed, like he didn't just *jump out of a damn helicopter!*

Garrett had already removed his parachute harness and protective gear, and was viewing the unfinished stadium with the discerning eye of a man who knew what he was looking for. Dad would compare this to a food critic who walked directly into the back of the restaurant before trying the food.

This was definitely *not* in the plan.

"Mr. Walker!" Dad shouted from the end zone, waving at the billionaire. He slowed to a light jog, then a walk, so he could catch his breath, and so the other board members could catch up.

I thought about all the athletes that would eventually run across this field and how much faster they would've closed the distance. We were a gaggle of overdressed businesspeople clumsily half jogging across the Astro-turf. We were probably the most out-of-shape bunch of people that would ever step foot out here, *let alone be running.*

Garrett turned to face us. He stuffed his hands in his pockets and waited for us to run to him. He made no motion that he was going to move or be inconvenienced in any way. Almost all of the stadium lights were on, which made the vision of him more imposing. He was one arrogantly confident man in a sea of green. It looked like the whole world was his stage.

What an ass.

The least he could do was meet us halfway. Who did he think he was?

Dad had a genuine grin on his face when I eventually joined him. Everyone else huffed and puffed behind us. Someone told the band to start, and they did. Fortunately for the musicians, they all had string and not wind instruments.

"What is it?" I asked Dad cautiously. I thought he'd be furious at the stunt Garrett pulled, instead he almost looked impressed.

"Smart. Very smart," he said, clearly to himself, through winded breaths. Dad cocked an eye at me when he saw me listening intently. "It's a power play. Not only did he shock us out of whatever preplanned spiel we had in mind by jumping out of the helicopter, but by forcing us to come to him instead of the other way around, he's making a statement even before the meeting begins. He's saying that—"

"*He's in control*," I interrupted absently as I studied Garrett who patiently waited for us to approach. With a nickname like the Grim Reaper of *whatever*, I imagined some gaunt, ugly guy, not a tall wall of muscle.

God, he was handsome.

His short brown hair was lightly tousled by the wind,

but still parted to one side. With broad shoulders and chest, and thick arms, he filled out his tailored suit and jacket perfectly. Not even Gloria's billionaire husband, Richard, dressed this well.

"For now." Dad winked at me. "Your old man's still got a few tricks up his sleeve. Keep up, Judy."

"Huh?" I asked, slowing down. I wasn't paying as much attention to Dad as I should have been. My brain could either ogle over this hottie *or* walk, not both. I forced my head down and sped up, reminding myself that this was business and that I had to be professional. "Yeah, of course!"

I wasn't great at being professional, but I was trying. I really wanted to show Dad that I could handle the responsibility this time. I wasn't about to let some rich guy screw me up. No matter how handsome he was.

"Mr. Sullivan?" Garrett asked, extending his hand.

"Yes," Dad said, the heaviness of his breathing from the run over had finally disappeared. "Pleasure to meet you, Mr. Walker. It seems you took the scenic route."

"I like to make my own way." Garrett had a hint of a New Zealand accent that straightened my spine. It wasn't just that his deep, sexy voice sent shivers through me, I also recognized it.

He used to be a big deal football player. I remembered his poster was hung up on my roommate's wall in college. It was the last thing I saw every night when I went to sleep.

He wore a few days of stubble over his chiseled jaw; it wasn't thick enough to hide the dimples in his cheeks, but it was dark enough to highlight his light, piercingly blue eyes.

Wait a minute. Why was everyone so hot and bothered over a football player? Last I heard, he quit playing five years ago. He was pretty, but he was a jock. I hated to stereotype, but playing football and running a stadium were completely different things.

How much could he possibly know about that side of things?

Garrett smoothly surveyed the crowd that gathered around him. Everyone said hello, some tried to introduce themselves fully, but no one could hold his interest long enough to get out their full title. Then, to my surprise, his gaze stopped on me. His eyes were the color of cresting waves and about a thousand times as deep.

"And who is this?" he asked.

"Me?" I gasped as if those waves were crashing over and drowning me. I didn't ask him to notice me. It wasn't like I was standing out in a crowd fangirling or anything; I was slightly behind both Dad and the other board members. For the first time in my life, I was at a loss for words.

"Uh, hi." I smiled, stammering the words out like a

gibbering idiot. Garrett patiently waited, giving me all his attention. The band played a little louder to relieve some of the tension, but that seemed to only make everything more intense between us. I felt like I was going to turn into a puddle under his gaze. "They call me Judy—"

"Don't mind her, Mr. Walker. She's my assistant." Monica stepped between me and him and took his hand. She was all wide smiles. "I'm Monica, the head of PR, and on behalf of everyone, we're pleased to have you."

His gaze lingered on me for another moment, then his lips hinted at a smile before finally shifting his attention to Monica and the rest of the group. My pulse was racing. It was then I realized I wasn't breathing and gulped in some air as quietly as I could.

What the hell just happened?

I don't get tongue-tied! If anything, I'm constantly putting my foot in my mouth for talking too much. Ah, that was weird. I've met famous people before, so what was so special about this guy?

They call me Judy?

I was smacked with self-doubt. No shit they call me Judy. Ugh, what else would they call me?

For once, I was glad Monica had cut me off, even if it was rude as hell. Horribly embarrassed, I slunk back a few steps. I gritted my teeth in something that I hoped would resemble a smile and tried to disappear.

With one look and a question, he'd turned me into silly putty.

"Are you hungry?" Dad stretched a hand back toward the luxury boxes where everything was set up for Garrett's arrival. That was where the meeting was supposed to start. "Can I get you a drink?"

"Let's start at your loading docks and work our way around." Again, Garrett had other plans.

"Oh, yes. Yes, of course. Right this way." I watched Dad's expression drop as we all started making our way to the gate beyond the southern end zone. He tried to hide his concern, but I knew him too well. His mouth pulled slightly to one side and brow furrowed. Dad was becoming less impressed and more worried with each step he took.

He wasn't letting on just how badly the stadium needed Garrett's money. He was our last chance at getting the funds we needed to build the rest of the stadium. If this fell through, a whole lot of people would be jobless.

It was hard to bear the weight of the pressure from the community.

"Reynobond aluminum metal composite material?" Garrett absently pointed up toward the third-tier seats

"Beg your pardon?" Dad asked.

"Your panels." Garrett raised an eyebrow skeptically. "Or are they insulated metal? *Or* are they a combination of the two?" Garrett's expression flattened as he watched Dad stumble for an answer, then look to the others. No one else could do more than rifle through whatever paperwork they brought with them and shrug.

Garrett might as well have been talking in a different language. So much for him being just another dumb jock.

"That's an awfully technical question," Dad replied. "I'll have to ask the construction company and get back to you."

"Who's running this project?" Garrett snapped back.

"I am." Dad mustered as much authority as he could, then went into some of the information he'd carefully memorized about how this was a community project that reflected the growth of Caldwell Hope and symbolized the next step in our town's evolution. There was a budding of pride in Dad's tone as he began speaking.

He got through about half of it before Garrett cut him off with a raised hand, telling him to stop.

"Hope and community aren't going to keep your stadium walls from collapsing, and it sure as hell won't protect you from a lawsuit."

The rest of the tour was much quieter, even the band stopped playing. Garrett would ask in-depth questions about construction, projections, finances, and anticipated sponsors. Sometimes Dad or Monica would have an answer, but it was never as thorough as Garrett would've liked.

The stadium project was a massive undertaking, with dozens of foremen and bosses overseeing hundreds of jobs. It was impossible for one person to know everything that Garrett was asking. I helped put together the informational package Garrett's people requested from us originally, and none of these questions were in there.

Did he come here just to make us look like a bunch of jerks? Hot or not, that was kind of a dick move on his part.

Was Garrett Walker always this cold?

I tried to remember what he was like when he was still playing football. I could've sworn my roommate showed me some of his interviews. We were both a little in love with him.

When we finally reached the stadium's massive glass and steel entrance, Dad had an employee come over with a wrapped gift atop a silver tray. It was slightly larger than a shoebox but was ornately wrapped in leather and cord.

"I know this is just an introductory meeting," Dad started, taking the box off the tray and dismissing the employee, "but as a token of our appreciation for you considering partnering up with us... well, here you go."

Garrett took the gift, pulled the cord and watched as the whole box opened up in his hand. It was an old beaten up football with a faded *A* stamped on one side.

Garrett abruptly blew out his breath as he turned the

football over in his hands. "I'm impressed. This is my old university in Auckland, isn't it?"

"It is." Dad beamed. "I'm not just the manager. I'm also a fan. I've had that in my collection for a few years now."

Garrett slid his thumbs across the long-since-glossy exterior of the ball, then brought it to his nose and sniffed in old memories of his past. He looked lost for a moment, like he was somewhere else entirely. The ball didn't seem to make him any happier, just distant.

I had to wonder, were they good memories or bad?

"So," Dad asked, attempting to wrap up the rocky business stuff on a high note. He'd probably try to get Garrett upstairs for small talk for a while. "Are you free tomorrow, or would you like to meet the following day to see the rest of the facility?"

"That won't be necessary." Garrett spoke slowly and to no one in particular. It was almost as if we weren't even there. "I've already made up my mind."

What? Already? He just got here. I didn't know much about big corporate deals, but I thought they were supposed to take more than twenty minutes. Dad blocked out the rest of the night for this and freed up a few more days later on in the week. This was a big deal!

"Woah." Dad chuckled, smiling nervously. "Are you sure? You haven't even seen the finished half of the stadium."

Like a man waking from a dream, Garrett's crystalline blue eyes came sharply into focus and snapped a gaze at Dad, then in turn he looked at the rest of us.

"My answer—" He calmly lowered the football. "—is no."

THIS IS THE PART THEY ALWAYS FUCK UP.

"You can't be serious. You just got here!" Paul Sullivan kicked off the wave of pleading and outrage while wearing a look of disbelief. I patiently waited for everyone else's shouts, complaints, and pleas to die down.

Contrary to popular belief, I didn't enjoy crushing people.

I didn't enjoy it on the field during my three straight years of MVP either. Just because I was really good at something, didn't mean I had to like it.

In the end, it didn't matter that I was the best in the business—you still couldn't take the championship with a bad team.

You wouldn't think it, but there was a surprising amount of carryover into the world of suits and ties. This stadium, for instance, was a *bad team*. I knew it before I stepped foot out that helicopter.

I didn't become the youngest billionaire *ever* by diving headfirst into bad investments.

"Here." I handed the football back to Paul, then turned to walk down the staircase that would take me outside to my waiting limo. "I'd hate to break up the set."

"Just wait a minute." Paul rushed after me. He laid a hand on my shoulder and in a hushed tone, he added, "Your father told me you'd at least hear us out."

I snapped an annoyed glare at his hand, which prompted him to immediately remove it.

"My father is the only reason I'm here." I paused, exhaled, then continued. "You're looking to sell naming rights for a stadium that's only half built. The long and short of it is if your town can't afford a stadium, then don't build one. Why would I want to put my name on something that might not get made?"

A silence washed over the group as I turned back around and resumed walking. I reminded myself that it's always best to leave after making my decision; nothing good has ever come from trying to explain my reasoning.

With a swish of air, the door closed behind me, ending my obligation to my father. I pulled my lapels a little tighter to protect against the chill. The sound of my steps on the concrete stairs down toward my limo rang out ominously, splitting the quiet, cold air of the dead winter.

Another wasted evening.

At least that tall blonde was nice to look at.

"Hey!" a voice cried out behind me.

I didn't bother stopping. I'd said everything I needed to say.

"Hey, *jerk*." The cute blonde from earlier jogged up and stepped in front of me, blocking my path. She didn't seem at a loss for words now. "Who the hell do you think you are?"

Her champagne-colored hair was neatly pinned in a French updo. She wore a white dress with gold jewelry that was a little too cocktail party for a business meeting. But who was I to talk?

My original attire was a *parachute*.

She had these sparkling green eyes, and they were flared with anger.

I studied the woman and could only smile in response. "You know who I am."

"Yeah," she said briskly. "Garrett Walker. You're some big, dumb jock who likes to ruin people. Good people who are trying to look out for their community. You obviously didn't want to be here with your ten-cent questions and your too-cool-for-school attitude."

"This... isn't how you're supposed to argue a point." I regarded her curiously and couldn't help cracking a grin at the way she spoke. *Too cool for school?* Was she sent out as some last-ditch effort, or did she chase after me on her own?

"I don't care. This might not matter to you, but this is our livelihood, and not just mine and my family's but the whole town's. Since the factories started moving away, Caldwell Hope has turned into a tourist-based economy. We need this stadium."

She was a few steps below me on the stairs, which made me tower over her.

"You shouldn't have built it in the first place." I'd had to harden myself over the years since Heidi. I did only what was necessary now. "That's not my problem."

"How can you be so cruel?"

"Cruel?" I cocked my head accusingly. In business, it was always better to tear the Band-Aid off fast rather than slow. I wasn't cruel. I was efficient. "I didn't tell you to overreach. You have a ski resort. That should be enough. When times are tight financially, you don't expand."

I took a step down, intent on passing her on the stairs, but she matched me by walking backward. Her shoes crackled against the blue deicer-covered steps.

"Y'know," she called out to me. Her foot skipped off her next step down, but she caught herself on the one below it. "I remember seeing an interview of you back when you played football. Everyone loved you. What happened to turn you so cold?"

"It's a cold world." I pulled my coat closed tighter. "I adapted."

That stopped her backward descent enough that I could finally walk past her.

"I understand now why they call you the Grim Reaper." Judy's disgusted tone bothered me more than I cared to admit. She reached out to shove me as I passed. "You're a cold hearted sonofa—"

Her shove knocked her off balance and sent her falling *up* the stairs. I was already too far away.

Without a moment's hesitation, I snapped a hand out and caught her by the wrist. Her glove was too loose and slid right off. I had to pivot, really reach in and wrap a hand around her waist. I caught her just before she busted her ass on the stairs.

It would've made for a great tackle.

Or a dance move.

"Are you all right?" I asked, pushing the weird sense of déjà vu out of my head. Had we ever done this before? No. That was impossible. I just met this woman. The only thing that mattered was that I had her now. She was completely safe.

"T-Thank you," she stammered, wide-eyed. Her breathing spiked with the abruptness of the fall, and an even quicker catch. "I mean yes." Her pulse was still racing, but her beautiful green eyes began to narrow. "I mean, what do you care?"

She tore away from me and pulled her glove out of my hand.

"I'm not a monster, Judy. I'm just—" That's when I noticed her one uncovered hand had a birthmark right above her thumbnail. It couldn't be, *could it?*

The blonde hair, her figure, the sound of her voice, the crescent-shaped birthmark, it all came back to me. It was her—*my dance partner from the masquerade.*

I didn't believe in fate or second chances. I never had to. I made my own luck. But could this really be a coincidence?

"Three days." I turned away from her.

"What?" Her hostility turned into curiosity.

"You have three days to change my mind."

FOUR

JUDY

"Judy!" Gloria waved me over to her table. The table, like most of the golf course clubhouse interior, was decorated in various shades of black, orange, and purple. Lace flourishes adorned the furniture. Elegant macabre paintings hung from the walls and small abstract sculptures were propped up on waist-high stands.

Halloween had come to Caldwell Hope and the town had never looked so classy.

The men mostly wore black waistcoats and trousers and white cravats, low vests, and white gloves. The elaborate dresses women wore were the black, scarlet, and violet of Victorian-inspired mourning, and the masks were inspired by the *Phantom of the Opera*. It was the

PG-13 gangbang of Mardi Gras, *Eyes Wide Shut*, and *Downton Abbey*.

I was loving every second of this!

"You're ruining it!" I spread my hands out wide, then let them drop to my sides, rustling my light blue tarlatan dress. I approached the table in a huff. "The whole point of a masquerade ball is so you don't know who everyone is."

"This isn't a car key party, Judy." Even through her mask I could see Gloria raising an eyebrow at me. "We're not criminals attempting a madcap caper. It's not against the rules to know who we're talking to."

"You're no fun." I shook my head at her, then turned to the woman who Gloria was chatting with. Molly was unmistakably pregnant in her indigo floor-length lace gown. "Molly, right? Luke's wife?"

"Hi." Molly smiled wide beneath her bright pink half-skull mask. "Don't tell me." Molly placed two fingers to her temple, closed her eyes, and rubbed her belly in feign divination. "Your name is... Judy."

I smiled. I knew *of* Molly and might've even seen her a few months back the night the King brothers played a concert at the record shop Gloria and I owned, but we'd never officially met.

"See?" I turned back to Gloria. "That would've been much harder to figure out if Miss Buzzkill hadn't spilled the beans."

"Speaking of personal titles." Gloria's lips betrayed her and curled up into a giddy smile as she brought up her hand for me to see.

"Get out!" I cried, grabbing her hand and sitting down next to her to admire the ring. I wrenched her toward me so I could get a better look in the low lighting "When?"

Gloria scowled at me for the sudden jerk and tore her hand away.

"Like two hours ago. I think he's going to make an announcement about it later." She couldn't be mad for long; she was still beaming from being proposed to. "I really hope he doesn't."

That made sense. For as take-no-shit as she was, Gloria hated being the center of attention in a group. She was the quiet mastermind type—basically my total opposite.

"Yep," Molly added. "She's *Missus* Buzzkill now."

I laughed. I immediately liked Molly and could tell we were going to be fast friends.

"Where's the rest of it?" I grabbed her hand again and turned it over. The diamond was small, like *regular* people small. "Richard is the eldest billionaire son of the King family fortune. There should be enough ice on your finger to sink the Titanic! What gives?"

Molly's eyes flashed at my audacity. Despite our working relationship becoming strained this past year,

Gloria and I had still managed to become good friends. She was the straight woman to my craziness.

"I'll have you know this was *the* ring Mercy Joel Oliver gave Missy Gladstone when he proposed to her. They died ten years ago. I have no idea how he got it." Gloria beamed, looking at us expectantly. "The band Twilight Son.... The bassist and the drummer!"

"Interesting." Molly nodded, trying to be supportive but obviously having no idea who Gloria was talking about.

I just shrugged.

"Heathens." Gloria shook her head. "Both of you."

The crowded dance hall made room for a couple across the way that was clearly in a fight. The large beefcake of a man stood stoically as the much shorter woman shoved a finger into his chest.

Whatever was going on looked messy.

"Where's Doug?" Gloria gave up all hope of us knowing the band she was talking about. There was more of an accusation in her voice rather than curiosity. She never liked my boyfriend, Doug.

"Playing cards and getting drunk with the waitstaff in the kitchen probably." I turned back to the other two ladies, visibly deflating at hearing my boyfriend's name. Between Doug and what I needed to talk with Gloria about, I felt like disappearing too.

"Forgive me if I'm being a little forward," Molly said

with hesitant care, "but that sounds pretty shitty. You're obviously looking forward to this event." She motioned at the intricacies of my mask and clothes, then glanced at Gloria for some kind of confirmation.

Gloria's lips became a thin pale line across her face as she slowly shook her head. She always told me he was boring, didn't pay enough attention to me and was kind of a jerk. I thought she didn't like him because he wasn't cool enough in her eyes, but lately I was beginning to see that she might have a point.

A song came on that sounded eerily familiar, but I couldn't place it. When I saw Molly's face light up, I figured it out. It was the song Luke wrote for her. He premiered it at our place, Black Rocket Records, during his band's reunion show. It was a sweet, catchy, and sorrowful tune that had just started to get radio play. Now the live band played it, probably as per special request from Luke himself.

The crowd near us on the dance floor parted and the rock star Luke King slid up to his wife on his knees, utterly destroying his fine suit pants in the process. In one breezy motion, he pulled off his mask—which was the same as hers, only his skull was black—and kissed Molly's belly half a dozen times before looking up.

"Hey, Mama." Unabashed love twinkled in Lucas's eyes when he looked at Molly.

My heart melted at the sight of it. I couldn't

remember one time Doug ever looked at me the way Luke looked at Molly.

"Hi, Luke," I said as coolly as I could. I still got a little starstruck whenever he was around. I *had* to get over that.

How do you get over men like the King brothers?

Richard was one of the most powerful businessmen in the country, and his brother Luke King was full-on rock star. They were Caldwell Hope royalty and heirs— sort of—to their now-deceased father's multi-billion-dollar fortune.

It had been a long couple of months. The town had only recently recovered from their insane rivalry. It was a case of billionaire takes all, in that whichever brother knocked a woman up first got all the inheritance for themselves.

"Hey, ladies." He brushed his long hair back and smiled pleasantly to both of us. Then he slid down his mask, gave Molly an evil grin, and carefully hoisted his pregnant wife into the air. Molly protested but was giggling through the whole thing. He seemed like the kind of guy who did this stuff with her a lot. "Sorry to interrupt." He carried Molly off. "My wife and I have a date on the dance floor."

Wow. I tried not to swoon. Richard King was hot as hell, but his younger brother, Luke.... *How is a man like that even real?*

"Hey, while we have a second..." I approached the sensitive subject tentatively. "...I want to talk to you about something,"

"What's up?" Gloria said, admiring her ring. She was still aglow from getting the proposal.

I hated to do this now, but I couldn't wait any longer.

"I... want to sell you my half of the Black Rocket Records."

"Why?" Gloria gave me her full attention. "We're just about to open a second location in San Francisco. Business is doing great right now."

Yeah, that's because I have nothing to do with the decision-making process anymore. I was co-owner with Gloria on paper only. That wasn't her fault though; it was my decision.

Gloria flipped up her mask to look at me more sincerely.

"Gloria!" I cried. "Masquerade."

"For fuck's sake... I'm leaving the mask off if we're going to talk like adults. The masquerade police can throw me in masquerade jail for all I care. This whole thing's stupid, and my fiancé owns the place, so I'll do as I please!" Gloria declared, loud enough for everyone in the area to hear her. Feeling less flustered, she turned back to me. "Now talk to me. Is this about the concert a few months ago?"

"No." And it wasn't... at least not completely.

Although not a day went by that I didn't think about my colossal screwup that almost bankrupted us. "It's just... I don't know."

Oh God, I don't even have the courage to say it out loud.

"Are you all right?" Gloria asked, leaning in. She lowered her voice and flashed her eyes down my stomach. Gloria was the only one who knew about my recent miscarriage. "There weren't any—"

"I'm fine." I shifted in my chair. Money talk always made me feel so awkward. "Never mind. Will you buy me out?"

"If this is about money, we can help." Gloria's black-rimmed eyes brimmed with concern. She was a good friend to put up with my craziness. "Seriously. You don't have to do this."

"No, I'm okay." I blew out my air and smiled genuinely. "I just need to separate myself from the old me and start over, y'know?"

Richard spotted us and sidled up next to his wife-to-be. He, of course, was dressed nicer than everyone. He wore an exaggerated gothic tuxedo with an opaque glass-and-silver half mask that must've cost a small fortune.

Only seeing them together did I realize they each wore one half of the same mask. That was really clever and adorable.

Doug accidentally left the one I made him at home

and came in wearing a paper plate monstrosity that he made in the parking lot. I'd spent a month working on them. All he had to do was bring it with him and he couldn't even do that. My blood boiled just thinking about it.

"The trick to a masquerade party is to keep the mask *on*." Richard pressed her buttons with a sly smirk.

"Oh my fucking God!" Her eyes went wide. She tore the mask off and slapped it on the table. "There. Now it's *on* the table."

I laughed.

"Hi, Judy." Richard was unfazed by her outburst. "Do you mind if I steal my fiancée for a dance?"

"Actually..." Gloria started, her annoyance falling away and concern again marred her face. "Judy and I were in the middle—"

"I don't mind at all." I smiled, offering a chipper tone and stood up. I honestly didn't want to keep talking about any of it. All it did was make me sad. "I need to go find Doug and harass him into at least one dance before he gets too drunk and makes another scene."

I didn't relish the idea of finding him, but I couldn't stay at the table with the happy couple any longer. I excused myself and made my way through the dance floor toward the kitchen.

Now that I saw it up close, I realized the floor was painted to look like a giant jack-o-lantern with gaping block teeth and glowing eyes. I was looking at everything except where I was going and crashed right into someone.

I bounced off the human wall, then tripped over my own heels. My face lit up in fright and shame. I was going to fall on my ass in the middle of the room, full of the most important people in the state. Senators, TV anchors, the mayor, actors, everyone was about to see me make an utter fool out of myself.

Then I stopped, hovering in midair for a moment. A pair of large hands had swept me up and pulled me into a dancer's embrace. Of course, I didn't recognize him because of the mask—which had two horns coming off the forehead, not like a devil but more akin to a Viking helmet. Whoever he was, he gracefully spun me to make it look like we'd been dancing together the whole time.

"That was close." His deep voice had the sound of a smirk in it. "Usually I like to meet my dancing partners before I try to pull that move off. Are you all right?"

"Holy crap. That was incredible!" I caught myself squealing and then forced a little more composure through my voice. "I owe you one, mysterious stranger."

My social savior had broad, defined shoulders. He didn't wear a suit jacket, just a French-cuffed, button-down white shirt, black pants, and a shiny red lattice-design covered vest. I could feel the hard grooves of his muscled back through both garments. It sent a searing thrill through me.

There was no way this guy wasn't an athlete.

His eyes were too perfect a shade of deep blue. I wondered if I could ever find that color in my oil paints at home.

"Yes." He smiled mischievously. "You do."

FIVE

GARRETT

Five Years Ago

"NICE MASK," I COMMENTED, WISHING IT WASN'T there. The half mask was porcelain with an accented tiara and peacock feathers shooting up from one side; it reminded me of something from the Italian Baroque period, but with bright and complementing colors. Among a room full of masks, hers stood out as more intricate and unique; it was easy to tell that love went into its creation.

I'd noticed her when I walked in but intentionally kept my distance.

I pulled her closer than I should have as we danced through a hole in the crowd. She was tall and had some curves about her. I liked that. I led her to a quieter section of the dance floor so we wouldn't have to shout at one another.

That and, if I got any closer to Lucas King, I was going to take his fucking head off. It was a good thing we had these masks on, or else both of us would wind up in the news again. I wasn't about to make a scene right now, not with his pregnant wife around.

Besides, after that blowout with Heidi a few minutes ago, the last thing I wanted was to draw more attention.

I needed a distraction.

"Thanks." My blond-haired partner smiled proudly. The look was enough to make me miss my next step. I hadn't seen genuine warmth like that in a long time. "I made it."

So she was beautiful inside and out it seemed.

Who was this woman?

"What happened over there?" she asked bluntly. "That woman looked pissed. Was that your wife?"

"Yes." I was a little surprised by her forwardness. "We're in a rough spot right now. I was hoping coming to this event with her would smooth things over, but it's only made things worse."

Heidi and I had been in a perpetual argument for months now. The smallest things set us off these days. I was on my way to becoming a billionaire, and still nothing I did was enough for her. It drove me crazy. I doubted she'd even come home tonight. Not like it would've been the first time.

I hated to think of where she might go, or who she might go to.

"Did you forget an anniversary?" she guessed. Her voice was light and bubbly. If champagne could talk, it would sound like her. "Or a birthday? You didn't run over the dog, did you?"

I wished it was that easy. Not the dog part though; that shit would be horrible. I wasn't about to tell a complete stranger that my wife just told me she didn't love me and was only staying because of our daughter.

"You don't have much of a filter, do you?"

"I— Shit. I'm sorry," she said. "My curiosity tends to get me in trouble. I can't help it. Aside from the King brothers, you're the only one here who looks larger than life. In the good way, I mean. I'm obviously not calling you fat!"

"I'd ask your name, but I guess that would defeat the purpose."

"Yes! I'm glad *you* get that." She glanced to the side, searching out someone; probably the person who didn't get "that."

"Where's your date? You can't be here alone." I glanced around this time, partly looking for some guy who was standing off to the side fuming that I was dancing with his girlfriend, and partly looking for my wife who might be doing the same, even though I knew I wouldn't find Heidi. I was doing what I could to hold things together for our daughter, but Heidi made it clear that she didn't love me anymore. I wish it hadn't come to this; Jackie deserved a chance at a whole family.

"That is a great question," my partner said sullenly. Then she chuckled, her hand slid across my back. "Doesn't look like it's our night, huh?"

"Who knows...." I spun her to the end of my arm, then rolled her back in. Her long blonde hair cascaded over my neck and chest, inundating me with its silky texture and flowery-smelling conditioner.

I greedily breathed in as much of her as I could. "Maybe it is *our* night."

She tittered nervously, thoroughly at a loss for words. I could feel her pulse race through her white gown. Her plunging neckline shifted when her spine went rod straight, as if noticing my touch for the first time.

She looked stunning.

I envied the poor, dumb bastard who this outfit was meant for; obviously the man was a fool for not noticing her enough.

Song after song, we danced in wordless closeness for a long while. It was perfect. For an hour or so, I could be a completely different person who was just dancing with a stranger.

"I feel like I should call you something," she said at last, once we drifted far enough from the rest of the crowd. The ambient lighting was strong enough where we were for me to finally see the emerald hue in her bright eyes. Not even the porcelain mask could hide her sparkling gems from me. "Not your real name of course, but something. Y'know?"

I didn't think she could get any prettier. I was wrong.

"Like a superhero name?" I let the absurd fantasy of it all part my lips in a grin. "Sure. Call me Grim. What do I call you?"

For bringing the naming concept up, she struggled with thinking of one. She had to know that I'd ask her for one as well, right?

"Rocket." She sighed, her cheerfulness tarnishing a bit. It made my heart ache with sympathy pangs.

"Fuck names," I said dismissively. I wasn't going to call her something that wounded her. "We don't need them. Just for tonight we'll be a man and a woman. To hell with everything else."

"I like that." She smiled again, pulling herself a little closer to me.

We chased the night away one dance step at a time, and for a while, I was able to let go of all the other crap on my mind. Football was so fucking all-encompassing these days. I felt like it was smothering me. Coach Miller was such an incredible prick about not allowing me any time to get my personal life together. I didn't know how much more of his shit I'd be able to take.

Far too soon, all the dancing was done. I held the mystery woman in my arms, not wanting to let her go. We'd slowly marched to the gallows of a decision. Part ways forever as strangers, or leave our broken worlds together.

It was so insanely tempting to do the latter and just leave it all behind.

"Thank you." She looked up at me with wide eyes. "It was a bad night until you came along."

"My pleasure." I softly kissed her hand. A tiny birthmark above her thumbnail caught my eye; it was in the shape of a crescent moon. I whispered into her ear, "You still owe me one."

My perfect dancer swayed lightly with anticipation. She wanted me to decide for both of us. The small portion of her face that I could see was eager, but also hesitant. I could only imagine what battles she fought in her head right now.

Thoughts of my newborn daughter washed through me and I knew that I never really had a choice at all. There was no way I could ever leave her, or be the reason she didn't have a full family.

My life was different now. My sacrifices were just beginning.

"Perhaps," I said, heavily discarding something truly unique and special. I dove desperately once more into her emerald eyes. "In another life we'd have gotten one more dance. Good night."

Then I left her forever.

SIX

JUDY

THE *HAPPY HALLOWEEN* SIGN HUNG FROM THE great hall's threshold.

"Isn't it December?" My voice was so distant that I briefly felt like a ventriloquist's puppet.

The ballroom floor was painted bright orange and black, like a jack-o-lantern with a great Cheshire grin. I was dancing in the middle of everyone. One wrong step, and I'd fall into the pumpkin's gaping smile and disappear forever.

Everyone wore these elaborate masks, but it wasn't a costume party. They all had on the suits and gowns of a formal evening party. I remembered loving the concept of it, but the name flitted away from me.

What was that called?

"A masquerade," the man I was suddenly dancing

with answered the question I'd never actually spoken aloud. "Where's your mask?"

He twirled me. I felt so small in his arms, so safe. In the mirrored far wall, I could see that I was the only one in the whole dance who didn't have a mask on.

What happened to mine? I know I wore one. I vividly remember making it myself. Where is it now?

"I don't know." Anxiety flooded me. This was a masquerade. I couldn't *not* have one. What was I going to do?

"Dance," the masked man said, pulling me closer. He was tall and broad, and his hands were strong like rough-hewn stone. He had the shoulders and thighs of an athlete; a large one at that.

Baseball or hockey maybe?

No... *football,* that was it!

It was glaringly obvious now. His mask wasn't a mask at all but a football helmet. He wore pads over his finely tailored suit. "Stick with me and they won't notice."

I believed him. How could they possibly see my face if I was dancing? I felt silly for not coming to that conclusion on my own. "But I don't know how to dance."

"I'll show you. Then you'll never forget." My partner masterfully led me around the dance hall. His every step was impossibly smooth and confident. He was amazing. Better than anyone I'd ever seen.

He moved me like a leaf on the wind.

I was his completely.

The music slowed and I got worried. What would happen if we stopped dancing? His body pressed against mine, and suddenly the pads weren't there anymore.

We were both completely naked.

"Our clothes!" I gasped, shivering. I looked to see if anyone was looking at us. No one seemed to notice.

"See?" he said, unconcerned. He still wore his helmet. The bars and straps somehow blacked out his face completely. That didn't make any sense. That wasn't how helmets were supposed to work. "They don't notice as long as we keep dancing."

Who are you? I stared into his icy eyes, which were the only attributes of his face the helmet didn't steal from me.

"You know who I am," he said. I heard the voice in my ears and in my mind. The look he gave me seemed to bore into my head, heart, and soul simultaneously. He didn't blink or look away, and neither did I.

I wrapped myself around his great chest, and let my head lull in the nook between his neck and shoulder. Without clothes on I was so cold, but he was a blazing furnace of warmth. *As long as I stayed there for the rest of my life, I'd be all right.*

He didn't hear that thought, or if he did, he ignored it.

He took my hand in a slow waltz, and slipped his leg

between mine. I felt the massive bulge of his cock on my inner thigh as he dipped me low. I closed my eyes. His cock was warm and hardening as it dragged across my leg. It melted the skin it touched, ruining me with renewed shivers.

My clit ached for his roughness. That yearning radiated out from my pussy until my whole body *demanded* to feel him inside me. I was wet and couldn't stop bucking up against him.

"It's been a long time since you were touched."

"A long time," I parroted distractedly. My limbs were turning into rubber. My body was giving in to him.

Despite my eyes being closed I could see that we weren't in the clubhouse ballroom any longer. We were in my old store, Black Rocket Records. My back and head still arched, I opened my eyes and looked at him. The rippling muscles in his arms and chest flexed to keep me from falling.

He gently lowered me onto one of the many small circular tables. The second he laid his fat cock on my swollen pussy, my legs trembled. It ignited a fire in me that only his cock could put out.

He leaned forward over top of me. To prop himself up, he slammed a fist down on the table so loud it startled me. "You've never been fucked by a man like me before."

"There are no men like you," I said, grabbing his helmet and tearing it off him.

Garrett Walker's face stared back at me. He seized the base of his cock and drove the impossible length into me.

I WOKE IN MY BED, SWEATING AND BREATHING heavily. Two of my fingers were pushed deep inside my pussy. My panties were embarrassingly soaked through.

Fuck, I was horny.

"No. No. Nonononononono...," I whined miserably. I spent the next half hour trying, and failing, to get back into my dream—to get back to my mystery dance partner. Eventually I gave up. "Dammit."

Ah! I hated this dream. What a frustrating way to wake up and start my day. Slowly pulling my fingers out past either side of my aching clit, my pussy clenched uncontrollably.

Oh, what the hell.

I breathed and slowly rubbed. Finding my rhythm and pressure, I summoned fresh thoughts of my dance partner's naked skin and huge cock. I imagined his sweaty, rough body lying on top of me, thrusting. I imagined the feeling of being filled up and having his pressure inside me, pushing me apart.... I came hard.

I laid there for a while.

What the hell was that dream all about? I understood

the sex part. Who wouldn't? But with Garrett Walker?

Garrett was an asshole. He was also a gorgeous world-renowned athlete. I doubted I was the only one thinking of him when they got off.

"Why the change of heart?" I asked myself, knowing I didn't have any answers for it. One minute he's all death and brimstone, then next.... *What did I miss?*

I sighed. Nothing made sense anymore.

I checked the time. It was still early. I had plenty of time until my father showed up and we went to meet *Mr.* Walker. Pretentious jerk.

The cool shower helped clear that horrible, sexy man from my head. I wasn't ready to put on big girl clothes just yet, so a clean pair of panties and an oversize T-shirt left here by one of the models I used to paint would have to do.

God, I needed to get around to laundry soon.

"Call Gloria, phone!" I demanded, placing my cell phone on my cluttered kitchen table. I cleared off enough space for a bowl of cereal and a glass of juice. Gloria was in my favorites so it would've been just as quick to touch the icon of the silly picture I had of her face and call her that way, but I liked ordering my phone to do things.

It made me feel like I was in charge of things.

"Hey, dude. What's up?" Gloria greeted me when the call went through.

"I'm freaking out is what's up." I poured cereal into a

bowl and brought my half gallon of milk to the table. "Also, hi."

I could hear the smirk in her tone when she asked, "What's freaking you out? Please don't tell me you're still mad about the latest season of *Arrow*."

"No! This is much more important. Although, yes, I am still upset about that show. It used to be *so* good and now—" I caught myself. My *Arrow* rant would have to wait. "Never mind. The fate of our whole town is resting on my shoulders, Gloria."

"Yeah?" Gloria asked distractedly. I could hear typing in the background.

"Gloria! This is important."

"Sorry... I'm just... wrapping up an email... riiiiight now. *And* sent. This is just a super busy time for us. We're opening a Rocket store in Hong Kong and— Shit, I'm sorry. You probably don't want to hear about this."

"No," I said "It's fine. Really." And it was.

Mostly.

Giving up my half of the company was painful, but *losing* it would've been even worse. Besides, Black Rocket Records was Gloria's dream, not mine. It was wrong for my father to have stapled me on to her project.

I just wasn't cut out to run a small business. I understood that now.

"Whatever, it's all boring shit anyway." Gloria dismissed the business stuff.

"Why are you working anyways? You're fit to pop any second!" I scolded.

"No, I've got another month. I know you know that."

"Just hammering the point home. Stop working! Go eat weird shit and binge-watch TV shows. I'm living vicariously through you and I feel exhausted."

"I'm not doing backflips, Judy. It's just a little admin work," she protested. "Tell me about what's going on with you?"

"I have to play tour guide for some wealthy investor and convince him to invest in the stadium." I idly browsed my small stack of mail as I ate and talked. Most of them were various bills, but a few were rejection letters from art galleries, which made me feel super awesome.

Not even my paintings were good enough.

"Invest how?" Gloria asked. "Last I heard your dad was just looking at selling naming rights."

"That or part ownership." I took a heaping mouthful of cereal and talked while chewing it. I'd never have done that around anyone else. "I dunno? Whatever will get us another hundred-million dollars." I swallowed my mouthful.

"Oh!" I abruptly remembered. "Did I tell you he jumped out of a fucking helicopter to meet us?"

"No... *seriously?*"

"Yeah, the guy's a total nut job!" I flung my rejection

letter across the room.

"Hey." Gloria's tone shifted. "You know we'd help more if we could." There was a pause on her end, then she added somberly, "Caldwell Hope is our home, too."

"I know." My voice was as full of sympathetic understanding as my mouth was full of Lucky Charms. Putting the majority of their wealth in a trust fund for their children was a great way to bring the King family back together, but it did come with some unforeseen drawbacks.

They couldn't afford to bail out their town in its time of need.

I finished my bowl of cereal as she caught me up with her latest pregnancy woes. The conversation was a bit bittersweet for me, but I was genuinely happy for them. It sounded like everything was really working out for them.

I casually put a few more strokes of color on a painting I was sporadically working on. It wasn't anything serious. I never had the inspiration for a real piece anymore, so I did little commissions here and there.

One corner of my kitchen was set up as a small art studio. It was nothing elaborate, just an easel, some additional lighting, plastic on the floor and surrounding wall —for when I got passionately messy—and a cleaning and paint station, which was a small square glass-topped table.

It wasn't much, but it was my favorite way to unwind. It was also why my house was a cluttered disaster. I was always working on one project or another.

"Which greasy old billionaire did you get stuck with?" Gloria asked flippantly, as the doorbell rang.

"Garrett Walker." I checked my melting Salvador Dalí wall clock. "Hey, I gotta let you go. Dad's here."

Weird. Dad wasn't supposed to be here for another half hour. I shrugged and went for the door. My condo was set furthest away from my other neighbors, so I didn't care that I was underdressed. And it was hard to care about being modest around a man who used to change my diapers.

"Woah, Judy...." Gloria suddenly sounded distressed. "Garrett Walker? The Grim Reaper of Wall Street?"

"Yeah. Silly nickname, right?" I undid the deadbolt and gave the door a heavy heave. For some reason, it always stuck in the winter. I shielded myself against the blast of snowy wind. The cold breeze whipped across my bare legs and up my double XL shirt, turning my braless nipples into hard little nubs of ice. "Hi, Dad. You're early."

"Be careful with that guy, Judy!" Gloria said in the background. "Garrett Walker is bad news."

I finally looked up from the initial blast and realized, much to my horror, it wasn't my father at the door at all.

"Hi," said Garrett Walker.

Of all the coffee shops in town, why did he have to pick the Rocket?

Garrett had walked off to make us coffees. I sat at a table along the back wall and bristled in the small mountain of clothing I wore. My stomach hadn't untwisted from the embarrassment I'd felt earlier. Ruthless corporate businessman Garrett Walker saw me prancing around in my underwear.

I wanted to hide under my comforter until I died of old age, but I couldn't. The whole town was literally depending on me to put on my big girl pants. How could I change the heart of someone who didn't have one in the first place?

Or maybe he lost it along the way somewhere.

I sank a little in my puffy white jacket, trying not to be noticed. It wasn't super busy, but there were still a few people mulling about the record and CD racks or flipping through some of the comic book stands. One young couple even sat on the small stage we used to use for live bands, and read poetry to each other.

I couldn't help but crack a small smile at seeing the place. It'd been years since the last time I was in here. Local art hung on the walls. The ones I remembered had long since been cycled out and replaced. That was one of the design elements I was most happy with. Whether it was painting, sculptures, or whatever, I loved the idea of sharing the work of local creators.

I was really glad Gloria kept that. Looking around, it seemed like she'd kept most of my design ideas. The place hadn't changed much in the years I was gone, except that it was doing much better financially.

Being back didn't hurt as bad as I thought it would, but despite it all, seeing Black Rocket Records doing well did make my heart ache a little. I wanted Gloria to succeed. It just reminded me how much better off she was without me.

"Judy?" a bubbly young voice asked from over my shoulder. I knew it was Penny before I turned. She had green hair this month and wore a big, wide-eyed smile and a prefaded Metallica shirt. It was good to see her. We hugged.

"Are you in college yet?" I asked. Penny hung out here with us after school every day, when we'd first opened, then she started working part-time when she was old enough. I did the math in my head. Penny had to be around eighteen or nineteen now. From the cleaning apron she wore, I could tell she was still working here.

"No. I'm taking a year off. I just need to figure myself out first. Student debt scares the hell out of me." She wiped down the small table then plopped down across from me. "What have you been up to? Did you go with Gloria to open a new store somewhere cool and exotic?"

"Hmm? Oh no. I don't— Gloria and I split ways a while back. Nothing personal. We still talk all the time. It just didn't work out. The business, I mean." I tried to put on a blasé attitude about the whole thing. Penny gave me a confused look. She obviously thought I was still part owner. "I'm up at the stadium working with my dad now; interning in the PR department."

"Oh." Penny's reply was a painful spike between my ribs. The look of sympathy she gave me afterward stung the most.

I wish that failure didn't still hurt so much.

"Just trying something new, y'know?" I chuckled, shrugging and trying to wave it all off. I was just making things more awkward. I struggled to keep the groan out of my voice and was mostly successful.

"Huh. I figured you'd have gone into design or something by now. Do you still paint?" Penny raised a perfectly manicured eyebrow, causing the piercing above her eye to catch the overhead light and sparkle.

"Yeah! Of course. All the time," I lied energetically. I hadn't had the time for that in a long while. I was trying to take my unfulfilling work seriously. I didn't want to let Dad down again.

Someday I'd feel inspired again.

"So..." Penny smiled, looking over her shoulder at Garrett who was finishing up with the coffees. "Who's the hunk?"

"*That* is none of your business, little girl," I teased, hiding the shallow depression that lingered in me like a bad cough I couldn't get rid of.

"Come on!" Penny leaned forward and whined at me. Penny was hopelessly forward with things. She got along with Gloria really well because of their shared bluntness when it came to telling everyone what was on their minds.

"If you must know, he's a potential investor, and this is a business meeting."

"Ohhh, swanky." She looked Garrett up and down as he began to walk back, two steaming coffees in hand. "Is he single?"

"No! He's not single," I whisper yelled. A flash of jealousy lit me up, but fortunately, Penny was too occupied to see it. "I mean, I don't know if he is, but you need to go."

What the hell was that? What did it matter if he was or wasn't? And why did I get so defensive at that? Great, now she put the thought in my head. *Was he single?*

"Okay, okay. I'm going." Penny got up as Garrett arrived.

They exchanged hellos, then Penny went to the counter to wait on a customer. She turned back around once she was behind him. She pressed her fingers to her chest and cooled her face by fanning herself with the other hand. All the while she mouthed the word "Hot" at me.

I stared daggers at her, hoping that anger would push down the flushness that was already swelling in my cheeks and neck.

It wasn't working.

"Take off the coat if you're warm." Garrett's eyes were intense and unreadable. His tone had a touch of mischief to it that was irresistible. He hung his jacket over the chair adjacent to us.

Garrett Walker is bad news. I rolled the statement around in my head like a sommelier might sip a fine wine.

"I don't mind." He stole a long glance at me and I felt nearly naked in front of him all over again. The look he gave me lit my skin on fire. "You look better out of them anyway."

Fuck! It was suddenly way too hot in here with this

bulky winter jacket on. Steam pulsed out of my turtle-neck like the spout of a kettle just about to boil. In my embarrassment, I had overdone it with the layers. With the coat and all my heavy winter clothes on beneath it, I looked like the Stay Puft Marshmallow Man. I really didn't want to take off any more clothes in front of him.

I hated the idea of letting him win.

He's just trying to rile you up. You're Caldwell Hope's ambassador!

People were counting on me. I couldn't afford to let him under my skin. Yeah, easier said than done. Gloria's warning to be careful rang out like a foghorn in my head. This wasn't just any businessman. This was the Grim Reaper of Wall Street!

"So, um...." I coughed, changed the subject, and glanced away. I stood up and quickly slipped the bulky coat off. If I didn't, I'd be a sweaty, uncomfortable mess in no time. Besides, by taking off my outerwear, he didn't *win* anything. The thermostat was set too high in here. I was just warm, that's all.

It had absolutely, *positively* nothing to do with the way his deep ocean-blue eyes flickered over me like the hottest part of a lighter flame.

"When's my father getting here?" I had texted Dad several times, but I didn't get a response. That wasn't surprising; he was notoriously bad at texting. If I was lucky, I'd get just the letter *K* or a question mark. For a solid week it was nothing but emojis. It wasn't even the common ones; it was the weird ones that no one ever used, like the Clipboard or the No Biking symbol.

"Unfortunately, Paul won't be able to join us."

"What?" My throat filled with sand. "Why not?"

"I asked him to give my assistant, Michael, the tour I was supposed to take yesterday." Garrett slowly mixed his drink.

"Okay...." My eyebrows turned upward as I tried to swallow all the questions I had with sips of my scalding coffee. Well, what the hell? What was the point of this then? Dad was the one who knew all about the stadium.

Thanks for abandoning me to the wolves, Dad.

"I'm not sure how much I can tell you about the stadium." I shrugged. "Dad is the real expert; I just work there."

"I know." Garrett leaned back in his chair, totally at ease. The wooden chair moaned under his weight, as if it were satisfied that he was there. Garrett was a man who was just as comfortable in long silences as he was in the chaos of a bone-crunching football play. "I don't want to talk about the stadium."

"I can tell you a little about the town," I offered eagerly, trying to fill the silence. I hated the long gaps in conversation and always rushed to lessen the tension. When he didn't immediately reply, I began educating him about the new school that was built and about the town's industry-heavy history. "Yelp has Caldwell Hope in the top fifty towns to watch in the coming decade. Between the ski resort and the new stadium, tourism is really starting to boom and—"

"Tell me about yourself." Garrett's commanding tone stopped me dead in my tracks.

"Me?" I asked more sheepishly than I wanted him to see.

Garrett slightly cocked his head, prodding me to say more. He sat in silence like a king on his throne, whereas I was crushed under it like a rockslide. It was suffocating.

God, how could one man have so much confidence?

"I don't think that's really relevant to the meeting." I tried to be evasive. Garrett's obvious power frightened me a little. He knew I was a painter. He knew that my house was a mess, and he probably knew that I used to own this place. That's probably why he brought us here.

Oh, and he knows what I look like half naked.

Knowing how he saw me made me cringe on the inside. I didn't like that he knew so much about me, especially since I didn't know all that much about him.

"You don't trust me?" he asked, completely unfazed.

"No." I couldn't contain my chuckle. I was the rabbit talking to the fox. The last thing I wanted was to get eaten.

Then again...

I'd be lying if I said his perfect teeth and wicked lips

didn't look tempting as hell. Every time he gave me *that* look, it went right through me like a lightning bolt. I thought about what would've happened if I let him in this morning instead of slamming the door in his face.

"Good." Garrett smirked, sending another lightning bolt directly into my pussy.

God, I had to stop being so attracted to this man.

"Ask me a question then." He casually sipped his coffee. He had a rebel air to him that could only come from his years as an athlete. "Anything you want."

Are we really playing truth or dare?

"Okay." I swallowed the old high school thrill that made my inner thighs tingle. One question for Garrett Walker. A million questions fluttered in my head; how could I narrow it down to just one?

What was it that changed your mind at the stadium? Why did you pick me to change your mind?

"Why—" I paused and swallowed. "Why did you jump out of that helicopter?"

I wussed out. How could I not? What would happen if I steered the conversation in that direction? I was here for the whole town, not just for me. I felt the crushing weight of responsibility again. Why did I have to be the one to do this? If I failed, what would everyone think of me?

Oh. Penny's reply stuck me in the ribs again.

Everyone already knew I couldn't even run a small business. What business did I have trying to save a town?

"Why not?" He shrugged, then glanced to the side.

Something on Garrett's face jerked me from my downward spiral. If I blinked, I would've missed it. There was an unmistakable hollowness behind his eyes. There was a flash of emptiness within him, like he was searching for something.

It was incredibly... human.

Adrenaline filled that hole for him, the same way painting did for me. I knew it was just a Band-Aid though. A painkiller. I couldn't help but wonder what happened to him that forged this hardened version of himself.

"You live in a tourist town." His face snapped back into this perfect mask that concealed all of his previous thoughts and emotions. "Do you ski?"

"I do," I said guardedly, still trying to give away as little as I could. I'd have asked him the same question, but the man jumped out of helicopters—odds were he'd been on a mountain before. "Are there any extreme sports you don't do?"

Garrett surveyed the room as he legitimately thought it over.

"I don't dance any more. Does that count?" He cracked a sexy smirk that made my nerve endings crackle. "Do you still dance?" He glanced back and snared my eyes. "I remember you were quite good."

Dance? How did he know anything about what I danced like? Again, he sent my mind spinning. I regarded him with utter confusion. I hadn't danced outside of my living room in years.

It was bright enough in here that I felt like I was really seeing him for the first time. I wasn't rushed or worried about a million other things, or caught off guard like when he picked me up this morning. All I could see was him. There was something about Garrett's eyes that filled me with some serious déjà vu.

Where had I seen them before?

An image floated through my subconscious like an ice cube bobbing to the surface of a chilled tea on a humid summer day. A Viking-style helmet mask with horns sticking out the front.

With that thought, came a surge of inspiration; it flowed through me like heroin. I was overcome with an urge to capture this moment. I wanted to paint. I didn't know why, but I needed to paint Garrett Walker.

Holy crap... the masquerade. That was the last time I danced. My eyes frantically looked him over. Like watching a puzzle get assembled in fast forward, every-thing dropped into place. The voice, his massive size, those stunning eyes.

I danced with the Garrett Walker?!

From across the table, Garrett's smirk deepened as he saw the sudden realization dawn across my face. The bastard was loving this.

"I—" My mouth opened to fill the void of silence, despite having no idea what I was going to say. How did I respond to that?

I was suddenly transported back to that party; all those mixed emotions cascaded through me, jumbling me up. Except this time, I knew who I was dancing with.

Thankfully, Garrett's watch lit up with an incoming call. He fished out a Bluetooth earpiece, slipped it into his ear, then answered. "Go ahead."

"Is she all right?" Garrett's playful smirk disappeared; it was replaced with an angry sternness that sent ripples of worry up my spine. Garrett's now ice-cold gaze snapped away from me; they narrowed and burned holes into the wall behind me. It reminded me just how quickly Dr. Jekyll could turn into Mr. Hyde.

That terrified me.

"I'll be right there." His voice lowered into a tone that could freeze everyone in the store. If we were in a room full of lit candles, they'd have all winked out in one go.

The Grim Reaper of Wall Street had returned.

EIGHT

GARRETT

"WHICH ONE DO YOU WANT, MY LITTLE COCONUT?" I held my daughter with one arm and gestured at the menu hanging outside on the wall of the ice-cream parlor with the other. I read down the list, watching her face light up when I said certain flavors.

It was a short flight and a long, sharp talk with the superintendent of Moses Thomas Elementary School. Their teachers were striking over salary disputes. Moses Thomas was the best elementary school in the state; I didn't like the idea of having to transfer Jackie somewhere else, especially after she finally started to make friends.

Friend, really. And that little girl only played with Jackie at school, never afterwards or on the weekends. Jackie didn't open up to many people. That was the long part of the talk. Even if the teachers hadn't started their protest, Jackie was in danger of being expelled for repeatedly lashing out in class and throwing tantrums.

Jackie's pediatric doctor recommended homeschooling, especially with the medication she was on. I couldn't do that to her. She needed to interact with kids her own age. It killed me to see Jackie acting out. She couldn't articulate it yet, but she'd been having a tough time since her mother—

"Black raspberry and... peanut butter!" Jackie threw her hands up, then followed that with a stern-toned, "With sprinkles."

"Are you sure you don't want just one first?" I asked Jackie, then turning to my assistant, I asked if they'd fed her lunch. He told me they had, then walked a few feet away to answer a call.

"I only want one." She gave me a confused look that made my heart melt. "I want half peanut butter and half black raspberry with sprinkles."

I decided against explaining the finer points of how scoops work and just bought her both.

"What do you say?" I asked, handing her the cup that had both scoops, the cone and sprinkles.

"I want a cone not a cup!" Jackie pouted, crossing her arms.

I set her down, then put both scoops of ice cream into the cone and handed it to her. "Better?"

"I didn't want a cup." Jackie refused to take the cone.

"We don't always get what we want, pumpkin. Sometimes we have to make compromises." I crouched down before her and took a bite of the peanut butter scoop. It was tastier than I thought.

"Hey, that's mine! That's not fair!"

Nothing is, unfortunately. "If you want ice cream, you're going to say you're sorry."

"It's Ms. Sullivan, sir," Michael said over my shoulder. He was holding up his phone, signaling that he had it on hold.

"Not now," I told Michael, then turned back to my grumpy daughter. "What do you say, Queen Jackie? Ice cream or no ice cream?"

"Sorry." She angrily reached for it, but I pulled it away before she could grab it. Then I raised my eyebrow and gave her a look she'd seen a hundred times. Finally she grumbled, "Please and thank you."

"Good girl." I handed the ice cream cone back to her and stood up.

"Sir?" Michael asked, hesitantly. "Sorry, sir, but she's insistent and she sounds... upset."

I felt bad for running out on her like that, but when it came to my daughter, everything else takes back seat. "Which one of my apologies did you give her?"

"I cycled through a few actually."

This was probably for the best. I knew I wasn't going to invest in the stadium. Why drag it all out for any longer? I shouldn't have even entertained it in the first place. Three days to win me over? What kind of fairytale narrative was I trying to recreate?

Even if she was the girl I danced with, it didn't matter. She could never possibly live up to the version of her I fantasized about for so many years.

This was business, I reminded myself. I wasn't going to hit thirty billion by my thirtieth birthday by making stupid emotionally charged decisions.

"Amidst several other grievances, she mentioned a promise you made about a dance. I don't really know how to answer that, sir."

I closed my eyes, trying to clear the image I had of holding her, the scent of her perfume, and the warmth of her skin, but the darkness only made that moment more vivid in my mind.

"What's on my agenda for the next three days?" I asked, wiping my forehead and smoothing my short hair back. Jackie sat quietly on a bench beside me eating her ice cream. She'd knocked the black raspberry off the cone and was nudging it with her foot.

Between Jackie, her school, business, and my own goals, so many things were going on right now. This was the worst time to go honor some promise I made to a complete stranger five years ago.

"Nothing that can't be moved around, sir." Michael browsed my itinerary on his phone.

Goose bumps climbed up the back of my head.

I remembered the biggest moments in my life. The phone call I received from Minnesota asking me to play for them, getting the call that Heidi was going into labor, my first endorsement offer that led into a stock share with a future billion dollar company, and signing the contract for my first casino. Every single one of those moments sent goose bumps up my neck.

Would this be one of those life moments?

If I didn't at least see what Judy was like, I might regret it for the rest of my life.

"Prep the jet. Have three days' worth of clothes prepared for Jackie and me, and keep me informed of the strike at her school." It would take a few days to get Jackie into a new school if I decided to go that route. Maybe a change in scenery would even do her some good.

"And Ms. Sullivan?" Michael busily took down my orders.

"Get a hold of my seamstress. Tell Tatiana I have a rush order for her."

"Very good, sir. A new suit?" Michael asked.

"No." I smiled softly, remembering the tap of our shoes as she occasionally stepped on my feet. "It's not for me."

NINE

JUDY

"Hello?" I asked, opening my front door. This time I was careful to be fully dressed. Garrett Walker would never take me by surprise ever again. For as angry as I was at him, my heart sank a little when it wasn't him at the door.

"Hi. Ms. Judy Sullivan, right?"

I answered with a nod, not able to hide the confused look on my face. Did I order anything from Amazon recently? Not that I could remember.

"Please sign here." The brown-clad UPS driver scanned a large box beside my door, pressed a few keys on his huge PDA from hell, then turned it around for me to sign with my finger above my name on the digital display.

Once I got the package inside I studied it for a few minutes before opening. It was from Tatiana Vargas,

LTD. I didn't recognize the name, but the packing tape had designs on it from all the biggest fashion magazines. Was she a clothing designer? No one ever mailed me anything.

What if it's a bomb!

I stepped back warily, then stopped and felt silly.

Who would want to kill me? I knew my student loan company was super tired of my missed and late payments, but a bomb is a little aggressive even for them.

This had to be some sort of mistake. I wondered how many other Judy Sullivans there were out there. It was a common enough name. Just a peek inside, then I'd try to find out who it was really for. I peeled the tape back and opened the box with the sheepishness of a little girl who stumbled upon one of her presents a week before Christmas.

I hung up the heavy bag by the coat hanger that came with it, then unzipped it.

"Holy crap...." I stepped backward. It was a midnight blue evening gown with a printed star pattern all over it. The glitter embellishments made the outfit *twinkle*. The plunging V-cut neck and back left little to the imagina-tion. And the viscose and silk material was so soft and smooth that it made my heart race and my mouth water.

Whoever this dress really belonged to had some sexy taste.

Then I saw the card.

Au Bon Chateau. Ten p.m. Tonight. -G. Walker
What an asshole.

"You must be joking." I huffed, planting both hands on my hips. He abandoned me downtown, then orders me to meet him. Just because he bought me a dress—a really, really nice dress—didn't mean I was his employee to order around as he saw fit.

I only mentioned that owed dance on the phone because I thought it might get him to remember that he promised to give me a few days to review the Caldwell Hope stadium deal. I didn't care how wealthy or brutally handsome he was, I wasn't going to be his booty call. This was about saving my home, that was it.

I zipped up the wearable work of art, then grabbed my coat. Dress in hand, I stormed out to his hotel. I was done playing by his rules.

"Sorry, Judy. He's not picking up." Deb hung up the phone. Deb had round brown eyes, and a casual, pleasant ease to her that I remembered since I was a child. She was a longtime friend of my mom and just happened to be working the concierge desk at the hotel Garrett was staying at.

"Is he even here?" I asked, draping the dress over the counter.

"Honey, a man like Garrett Walker is hard to miss." Deb raised a slightly over-shaped eyebrow that gave her a look of constant surprise. "He's probably just in the gym. That's where he spends most of his time while he's here."

The gym, theater, and executive suite floors were access card only. I didn't own the building like the King family. The only way I was getting up there was if I was with him or if he was expecting me. Neither was going to help me right now.

"I really need to talk to him. Can you... let me in?"

"You and a hundred other women," Deb laughed. "I would love to help you, hun, but I could get in a lot of trouble.

"Deb, please. It's important. Really." *And it was.* If I could show up unannounced, then I could even the playing field. I could show him he didn't have *all* the power and that I wouldn't be pushed around.

She glanced up at the discrete camera that watched us, then pulled her mouth to the corner of her face. The look told me she felt bad, but there really was nothing she could do. "What do you have there? Is that a dress?"

I sighed. It was a long shot. I draped the dress over Deb's side of the counter and let her unzip the front of the plastic protective cover.

"Oh my gawd. Is that...?" Deb slid her fingers along the hem, looking for a tab. "It is!" Her eyes went wide and her tone hushed. "Sweetie, this is a fifty-thousand-dollar dress! Did Garrett give this to you? Is that why you're here?"

Fifty-thousand? My family had always done well, but I never dreamed I'd have a dress—or even a car—that was worth that much. That was insane.

"Yes," I said. "Now you see why I have to go talk to him."

"Who am I to stand in the way of love?" Deb winked, zipping the cover back up. She handed me the dress back. "Now you run along, and please don't try to bother Mr. Walker... who's at the gym right now... on floor twenty-four."

"Oh no, it's not like that—" I began to protest while dragging the dress over to me. Then something small and rigid in the bottom of the bag slapped against my leg. My eyes lit up.

She slipped me a key card.

Before I could thank her, she shooed me away with a big grin, then greeted another customer.

Deb, I friggin love you! I took the hint, while pretending to be disappointed at being denied like so many other women, and went to the elevators. Once inside, I fished the key card out of the plastic bag and used it to get to the gym level.

I looked into the mirrored elevator walls psyching myself up for the meeting with Garrett. *Okay, be mad!* I pointed at the mirror and shouted, "You think you can buy me like a whore?"

Okay, too much. Bring it back a little.

"I don't want your bribes. I want— No, I *deserve* a fair deal."

Better. Confident, not crazy.

The elevator doors opened to a glassed-in foyer area with towels and an empty employee desk. Beyond the door and glass walls of the foyer were rows of free weights and exercise equipment. It was all right there and it went on forever. I thought the gym was going to be on floor twenty-four, but it turned out the entire floor was the gym.

Eerily, the floor seemed completely empty. It was the biggest hotel in our town, surely at least someone would've wanted to pop down for a quick jog. I walked past the foyer doors and picked up the subtle scents of chemical cleaners mixed with the bleach from the pool.

The weirdest thing by far was the music. "Circle of Life" wrapped up, then the song from *Aladdin* started playing, the "I will show you the world" one. Who the hell worked out to Disney music?

During the lull between the two songs, I heard a distant voice and made my way to it. As I rounded the enclosed pool, hot tub, and steam room areas, I realized the voice was that of a young giggling girl and she was counting. There was also another sound that was out of place for a gym.

"Ten." Bounce. "Eleven." Bounce. "Twelve." Bounce.

When I poked my head around the last corner, I found that the noise came from a rubber ball, one you'd use as a kid to play dodge ball. The girl couldn't have been more than six or seven. The ball would land a few feet in front of her, bounce, she would catch it, then count and throw it back to—

Oh my....

Garrett Walker had his knees bent and was hanging upside down on a pull-up bar. He was shirtless with his arms stretched out toward his daughter. He caught the ball, then did a sit-up. His abs tightened, his chest flexed and crushed together, and the muscles that ran up his sides bulged and heaved as he raised himself upright for another repetition. Once he tapped the ball on a bar high above his knees, he lowered himself back down and tossed the ball to his daughter.

He looked so much different than in my dream.

I remembered that he was in great shape from the interview I saw of him a long time ago, but seeing a professional football player in person was... wow. All he wore, aside from thin Converse shoes, was a pair of loose-fitting fitness shorts that, due to him hanging upside down, rode up to where his legs came together. Although his cock was completely covered by the fabric, everything else was a feast for the eyes.

He was over two hundred pounds of sweat-dripping sexiness. I had to check a few times to make sure my tongue hadn't rolled out of my mouth.

I figured he had a few tattoos, but I'd never have guessed it was *that* many. He had two scythes across his chest, above an explosion of color and imagery that stretched down both arms and across his back.

It was beautiful; I could study both the art and the canvas for days.

"Eighteen!" the girl excitedly exclaimed. "Only three more!"

"Great job, baby!" Garrett smiled at her so sweetly that it immediately dissolved all my anger against him. When he wiped the sweat from his eyes, they sparkled. It was easy to see how proud he was of his little girl. "You're going to be the best little athlete ever, you know that?"

"Daaaad." His daughter lit up with embarrassment. *Oh good, it's not just me he can do that to.*

"Eighteen," she repeated, then threw him back the ball. He caught the ball easily in one of his large, strong hands.

"Are you trying to trick me?" he asked her, playfully stern. She laughed. "What number comes after eighteen? Twenty-five?"

"No." She smiled knowingly. Her breath whistled through a missing front tooth. "That's too high!"

"Five?" Garrett held out his other hand, opening his fingers one after the other until all five were stretched out.

I leaned against the wall, loving every second of this. The Grim Reaper of Wall Street playing catch—granted, a more extreme version—with his daughter while Disney songs played over the gym speakers.

How friggin' cute was that?

Maybe he wasn't the man everyone thought he was. Maybe there was more to him.

I felt like I could've watched this all day, and maybe I would have, if he hadn't glanced in my direction. His smile faded as he raised an eyebrow at me. The look put me back on my heels.

It abruptly occurred to me that I was intruding on a private moment with him and his daughter. He probably still got stalkers all the time.

But I wasn't stalking him. I came here to yell at him. The little girl followed her father's gaze and waved at me. "Hi! My name's Jackie. Do you want to play with us?"

Garrett glanced back at her, then gave me a concerned look, which looked especially intimidating while he was hanging upside down. In one smooth motion, he flexed his taut, cord-like thighs and flipped down onto his feet. With moves like that, it was impossible to picture him as anything but a top tier professional athlete.

"No, sweetie," he told Jackie, gently handing her the ball back. He then walked toward me, grabbing a towel off a nearby shelf and drying his face along the way. His face was set and his steps were deliberate. Every foot closer made my heart race faster. He was not pleased that I was here. "Our new friend is just leaving."

"I wasn't stalking you!" I blurted and stepped back reflexively as he reached me.

"How'd you even get in here?" he asked towering over me. Garrett's tan, bulging body glistened as he addressed me. The heat rolling off him hit me first. His body smoldered like a blast furnace; it seemed to suck all the oxygen out of the room, making it hard to breathe.

Then his aroma enveloped me. Even his scent had layers. It was the musk you only got through exercise or sex, plus the tang of steel that he'd been pushing, pulling, and hanging from. Beyond that was the faint pleasant whiff of cologne that hadn't fully been washed off.

It was the manliest smell I'd ever been exposed to. If he'd been around burning wood at all earlier, I'd have swooned and collapsed on the spot.

"I'm an important figure in the community," I lied. "I have friends in high places around here."

Why was I lying? Because *"I snuck in because the desk clerk thought we were in love"* sounded too crazy even for me. I looked around and tried to defuse some of the tension. "Where is everyone? You'd figure a gym this big would be a little busier."

"I like my privacy. I rented out half the hotel so I'd have *exclusive* access to the gym."

"Well, not *exclusive*, if you want to get technical. Your daughter's here too—"

"Why are you here right now, Ms. Sullivan?" Garrett crossed his monstrous arms, which made the scythes that ran up his forearms heave and twist. The motion puffed his chest out and nearly doubled his already large silhouette.

Jesus, no wonder he earned the Grim Reaper nickname on the field. He had the innate ability to be terrifying while playing a sport, or making a million-dollar deal.

"Why am I here?" I repeated the question in awe of the god that stood before me. I felt like I was made of glass and might shatter at any moment.

Then I remembered the stakes and did my best to squash the weakness in my knees and the tingling in my lower belly. I looked up at him fiercely. "You're kidding, right?"

He narrowed his eyes, a glint of surprise and confusion in them. He probably thought I'd buckle like so many other people had.

"You abandon me while out at a meeting, then try to

weasel out of our deal." When I didn't turn to ash under *the* Garrett Walker's death stare, I stood up a little straighter and continued, "I had to all but blackmail you to get you back here.

"And what is this?" I smashed the bag into his incredibly well-defined, sculpted— I shook the thoughts out of my mind. *It was a regular chest,* I reminded myself. A big, dumb, handsome regular chest, that was all. "An apology? A payment? I don't want anything from you except what we agreed on."

I did want the dress.

"I want my meeting and I want you to take me seriously." I mustered up as much authority as I could.

"And your revenge for not taking you seriously is harassing me when I'm with my daughter?"

"I wasn't ogling you!" I paused. *Shit, he said harassing, not ogling!* "I'm here to make sure you didn't bail on me again. I'm tired of waiting on you and we're not going to that restaurant because I hate French food."

I had no idea if I hated French food, but I wasn't going to tell him that.

Garrett cocked an eyebrow at my display, unfolded his arms and placed them on his hips. I couldn't tell if that was a good or a bad sign. God, this guy was hard to read.

"This is your town." Garrett shrugged, unconcerned.

"You're the one who wants *my* help so why don't you pick the next place?"

"I will." I gave him as much attitude as I could scrape together, which wasn't much unfortunately. "We're doing lunch instead, so...." I waved a hand at his gorgeous torso.

"Lunch?" Garrett asked, cocking an eyebrow at me.

"Is that a problem, or are you going to run away on me again?" This time I crossed my arms, despite still feeling as fragile as a porcelain doll on a roller coaster.

"If this honors the verbal contract, then fine," Garrett flatly stated, then he turned to his daughter and was warm as fresh baked pie as he said, "Let's get you upstairs with Bridgett, sweetheart. I have to go to a meeting with our new nosy friend here."

"Aw, Dad," Jackie whined, stomping over to us. "You said we could play today! You said you didn't have work till after dinner."

"Sorry, Jackie, but sometimes plans change." Garrett glanced back at me.

Seeing the disappointment in Jackie's face made me immediately feel awful. She was having so much fun with her dad, then I came and ruined it.

"Hi Jackie. My name's Judy." I bent forward and shook Jackie's hand. "You want to see a magic trick?"

She nodded, her face brightening a little. When I let go of her hand, I put my thumb between my knuckles and pretended it was hers. "Whoops, I stole your thumb!"

It was the world's dumbest magic trick, but it put a smile on her face. It also managed to rob some of the sternness from Garrett's expression as well.

"No, you didn't." Jackie laughed. She checked her hand just to be sure.

"You want to come with us to lunch, Ms. Jackie?" I asked her.

"I don't think that's a good idea." Garrett was quick to interject.

"Why not?" I looked up at him "I happen to know a very classy place that welcomes children."

He gave me a skeptical glance, then crouched down next to his daughter. "It's up to you. You want to come with us?"

Jackie nodded.

TEN
GARRETT

"This is your idea of classy?" I asked, taking off my long wool jacket and draping it over my arm. Jackie squirmed as I pulled off her puffy coat. I placed her hat, gloves and scarf in her coat pocket, then handed the heap of clothing to the boy in his late teens who ran the coat check room.

Crazy World Adventure Park was a renovated big box store plot turned gaming complex. The theme of the company was child-friendly oversize monsters run amuck. There were molded plastic statues everywhere. One was of a T-Rex anxiously trying to hold a putter near the glow-in-the-dark mini golf course. An octopus played three separate video games simultaneously in the arcade, and a unicorn escaped from the merry-go-round so that children could take pictures on it.

"Look, see? There's a dress code and everything.

Formal attire only." Judy pointed over to the twelve-foot-tall pink gorilla sculpture by the entrance of Crazy World. It was dressed and posed to look like the famous picture of Marilyn Monroe pushing her white dress down while standing on the steel grate, only to have the wind push it back up.

Judy shrugged off her winter gear and flashed a big grin to Jackie, who started giggling right away. The joke went over Jackie's head, but it didn't matter. It was amazing how quickly those two took to one another.

That worried me.

"Look, Dad! That's silly," Jackie yelled gleefully as I picked her up.

"Let's get you some food, so you have energy to play." I smiled warmly at my daughter and carried her over toward the restaurant. Turning to Judy, I asked, "I'm guessing this place doesn't have a Michelin star?"

"No, but we can grab a pack of the gold star stickers from the gift shop and put them on your plate if that'd make you feel better," Judy joked, obviously feeling more comfortable in a casual setting. Was this what she was like normally?

I remembered her being lighthearted and giddy at the masquerade, when we were just two dancers. Despite all the drama happening in both our lives at that time, it was just her and me, and music. It was amazing how such a brief moment could stick in your head so strongly.

"Molly!" Judy's smile deepened as she waved to someone behind me.

Molly was a tanned, olive-skinned woman with dark auburn hair and a knowing smirk. She sat at one of the many picnic style tables with a feast of food in front of her. Molly waved back while trying to get a little boy—who looked to be around Jackie's age—to eat. The boy fidgeted and pouted as he made a general mess of half a hot dog and mustard on his paper plate.

"No. You have to eat something first. Just one thing, that's all I'm asking," Molly said to her son, then looked up at us, exasperated. "I hope you don't mind, I ordered us a few things."

"A few things, Moll? Did you leave anything for the rest of the families here?" Judy hugged Molly.

What families? Like the coffee shop yesterday, this place was nearly empty as well. Granted it was a weekday, but it was still eerily empty. The Monster Mash played over the speakers. The music did little to lighten the sense that this adventure park, like Caldwell Hope as a whole, was a rusting clock and its gears were slowly grinding to a halt.

Judy then introduced us to Molly and her son, William. We sat and joined them for food. The children finished eating quickly but had to wait for us, so they created a game where William called out whether it was daytime or nighttime. When it was nighttime, Jackie danced next to the table. When he shouted out daytime, she laid next to me on the bench and pretended to sleep. Back and forth it went.

"Thanks for joining us, Moll. It's been ages since I've seen you and Luke! How've you been? Are you still working at the school? Oh! Luke is on tour, right?" Judy asked a torrent of questions in rapid succession.

Over the small talk, I noticed when Judy got excited her mouth kicked into overdrive. She had this youthful energy about her that I really liked. Molly just chuckled as if having forgotten how much Judy talked.

"We're good. Lucas just got back from Berlin, Germany, yesterday; they *finally* let him play there again. He's meeting with his publicist right now." Molly swallowed her last bite of the still half-full mac and cheese container, then dropped the fork and pushed the plate away defeated. "Will starts kindergarten soon. I'll probably work a few hours at the elementary school during the day. I do miss the kids."

"So, Mr. Walker, have you made up your mind yet?" Molly asked. "About our little town."

Molly King was the wife of billionaire Lucas King, of whom I wasn't the biggest fan. Still, Lucas's father, William, put Caldwell Hope on the map in a lot of ways. It was apparent that the King family still loved this town.

But if they did, then why not back the stadium themselves?

Why not save the town they loved?

I finished my last chicken tender and licked the honey mustard off my finger. The food wasn't particularly good, but it did have a nostalgic feel that I appreciated. It reminded me of my grandfather taking me to the carnival when I was young.

"Not yet." I smiled charmingly. "Ms. Sullivan here is still showing me around." When Molly turned to wipe some food debris off her son's face, I looked at Judy; my eyes searching her, *studying* her. "She's full of surprises."

Judy blushed under my gaze. She stood up and addressed the kids. "Let's go play some games!"

They cheered in response. After we cleaned up, we made our way to the arcade. Jackie and William became fast friends, challenging each other to game after game. After an hour of playing chaperone, Molly shooed us off to have some fun. She promised to watch the kids and, resolving not to wander too far away myself, I reluctantly agreed.

This was supposed to be a meeting after all.

"We gotta try this one," Judy said in exaggerated disbelief. Playing with the kids had loosened her up tremendously. She seemed less rigid and worried, and in her excitement, she reached for my hand to pull me toward NFL Blitz, a football video game. She caught herself right as our fingers touched, spreading to interlace with each other like it was the most natural thing in the world. She abruptly pulled away, her smile faded as if she realized she just made a mistake. "If you want, of course."

That two-second touch with Judy packed more of a spark than spending a whole night with most women. I longed for something as simple as holding her hand. I'd never felt that way, not even with Heidi.

"Only if you're not a poor loser." I slid a hand gently across her lower back, guiding her to the machine. I felt her breath spike through her blouse. "You do know I played this professionally right? MVP and all that."

Next to the turtleneck, khakis, and winter layers she wore yesterday, today's simple purple blouse and slacks looked like a bikini. And that was a far cry from how I'd seen her that morning. The image of her half naked answering the door was one I carried with me whenever possible. My cock always stirred at the memory of Judy's nipples poking into the cotton shirt, hardening at the sight of me.

"You're on." She loaded the machine up with tokens and tentatively nested in next to me.

Standing so close to her as we played forced me to push myself against the waist-high game to keep the bulge in my pants under control. The hair on my arms stood up as our forearms touched.

Damn. It'd been awhile since I felt like this. It wasn't just attraction to Judy. I was attracted to a lot of women. It was something more three-dimensional, something realer than just sex.

Although, I did want to fuck the shit out of her, too.

"Ha!" She turned to me with more smugness than I'd seen in her yet. The screen lit up proclaiming player two was the winner. "In your face!"

"It was a tough game...." I put on my press conference face and voice tone, then addressed Judy like I would a room full of reporters after a game we'd lost. "I'm proud of all my guys. They laid it all down out there on the field. The other team just wanted it more. They've got a good coach. She's a real hard-ass. And is quite the handful." I leaned around her to check out her ass. "More of a double handful."

"Hey!" Judy's eyes became the size of saucers.

"And, uh yeah, we look forward to the rematch," I continued. My smirk broke into a chuckle when she playfully slapped my shoulder. "No further questions."

We played again, and again she beat me. Several more games and a few hours seemed to slip by with neither of us noticing. Molly contently read a book and watched the kids play while Judy and I challenged each other to nearly every game we came across. I hadn't had fun like this since I was a kid. Maybe it was because the arcade was mostly empty, save our group, or how casual it all felt, but there was definitely a magic in the air that afternoon.

I'd never seen Jackie play and laugh so hard. She and Will had really hit it off. When they weren't playing a game, they were chasing each other around, creating their own games. I'd always been envious of how quickly children could become best friends.

"I believe the final count puts me ahead by two. MVP, huh?" Judy smirked and slid the plastic gun into the arcade game's holster like a victorious cowgirl after a deadly shoot out. We stood side by side at a zombie house shooting game. The shrill cackle of the Game Over screen just started to cut off and reset. Judy's beautiful emerald eyes twinkled with pride and something more. "I hope you're better in real life."

"I'm not just an MVP on the field." I leaned in, giving her bedroom eyes and the hint of a smile that promised only trouble and a good time. She was still close enough that I could smell the citrus from the orange soda on her breath. I hadn't had a soda in years, but I craved a taste of it more than anything.

We shared a moment—a lull between words and obligations. I knew the moment like my own reflection in the mirror. For just a second, we were completely alone. Just like we were that night we danced together. We couldn't come together that night, but today... there was a hole in time that could only be filled with a kiss.

A *first* kiss.

"Dad!" My daughter tugged at my leg and, just like that, the moment passed.

I sighed, switching gears hard. There was one thing in life even more important than moments like these. I dropped into a crouch to talk to my daughter. "What is it, my little coconut?"

The music clicked off and some of the lights in the empty parts of the building started snapping out. Closing time already? We were just having lunch, weren't we? I couldn't believe how fast time flew with Judy.

"Will invited me over to play at his house and his mom said it was okay. Can I go play at Will's house? Can I? Can I?" Jackie hopped up and down excitedly.

"I don't know...." I thought it over.

I was torn. Jackie needed friends, but what happened when we left Caldwell Hope? I could be in boardrooms all day, but the toughest decisions I'd ever had to make were as a parent.

"It's no bother for us." Molly tussled her son's sandy blond hair as she walked by. "Lucas always makes too much food. Judy knows the way. You can...." Molly trailed off, glancing at Judy who was uncharacteristically quiet. Judy coughed, trying to hide the faint glow about her from our near moment. Molly smiled. It was a small thing, but it saw right through Judy's charade.

"We'll set a few extra plates if you feel like joining

us." Molly hefted her purse and gathered up her son's things. I shook her hand and the kids hugged their goodbyes.

Molly hugged Judy and carefully whispered something into her ear.

What did she say?

The dinner offer did not sound appealing. I had no inclination to meet Lucky Luke again. Once was too many. I went to that show that banned him from Berlin. The way I saw it, he got off easy for what he did.

"Can we, Dad? Can we, can we, can we?" Jackie latched herself to my leg. Her face beamed as she looked up at me, a big gap-toothed smile on her lips. "Pleeeeease."

If I had a weakness, it was certainly my daughter.

"Sure, coconut." I sighed. That Germany show was a *long* time ago. We were both very different men now. I doubt he'd even remember me. "Only for a little while."

If there was one thing I couldn't stand, it was strained small talk with people I didn't like. But looking at Jackie's gleeful, chubby face, how could I say no to her?

ELEVEN
JUDY

"Well?" Molly poured me another glass of wine. It was amazing how she could hold the same smirk for hours without cracking.

Garrett had to stop back at his hotel for a few hours before meeting us for dinner, so I just rode with Molly. She'd been passively insufferable the whole time.

"What, *well*? Why are you well-ing?" I snatched the full glass from her eagerly and took a sip. "There's nothing to *well* about."

Molly raised and lowered her eyebrows, then deepened her grin ever so slightly, but otherwise didn't say a word.

Luke chopped veggies on the marble island, humming a quiet tune to himself. He was working out a new song in his head. He'd been bursting with inspiration for a while now. Luke had put out a new album each year, like clockwork, since they had William.

It was obscene how jealous I was of Gloria and Molly, with their stupid perfect lives and stupid happiness.

"Do you like the wine?" Molly asked innocuously. The wine glass covered part of her perpetual smirk. *God*, even her eyes smiled smugly!

"Ahh! You're so nosy!" I cracked under her relentless glare. "Yes, okay. I like him. I hate that I do, but I can't help it! Happy? Are you happy now, you horrible, horrible friend?"

I put the glass down, and ran both of my hands over my face and hair as I slumped into their bar on my elbows. I hated hearing it out loud. It sounded so hopeless and silly.

"Ha!" Molly's smirk became a wide toothy grin. "I knew it. You were glowing so hard at the end that I could've plugged my phone into you and gotten a good charge."

"The Dark side is too strong with you."

Molly cackled evilly and tapped her fingertips together rapidly.

"Frustrating, isn't she?" Luke set down a platter of mixed veggies and dip. He winked at his wife, then kissed her on the cheek as he passed to check on Will.

"What the hell am I going to do, Moll?"

"Please." She held up a hand stopping me. "Use the full title, *Darth* Moll."

"This is serious," I whined, and slapped the table like a child throwing a temper tantrum. I took another sip of wine and pulled myself together. "I can't fall for him. I *need* something from Garrett. The fate of the whole town rests in his hands."

"That's a bit much." Molly grabbed a carrot stick and swirled it around in the dip.

"It's not." I snatched the carrot away from her and chomped down on it. "Caldwell Hope is in rough shape."

"Richard and Lucas are doing what they can." Molly's tone went somber. She saw it too. The graduating class at her school this year was at an all-time low. She was worried, but she was a master at not freaking out.

Me on the other hand....

"I know. I know. And that's great, but they're just a Band-Aid. Jobs need to come back, and the only way that happens is with this stadium. I feel selfish even fantasizing about him. I'm in way over my head. I should ask someone else to show him around."

Richard and Luke King were *technically* billionaires, but not really. They decided to pass on their father's inheritance to their children instead of taking it for themselves. That left them with only what they'd made for themselves, which was still a lot of money but nowhere near a billion dollars. They helped with small loans and charities as much as they could, but there was only so much they were able to do.

Gloria told me about it once and it made my head spin. I couldn't imagine giving up that kind of money.

"Didn't he expressly say that it had to be you?" she asked.

"Yes. He's tormenting me." I gestured loosely enough that I spilled a few drops of wine on the marble-topped bar.

"You know he's into you, right?" she asked, dunking a piece of broccoli into the dip. I snatched it from her a second later. "Come on!"

"Of course I know that." I ignored her indignant shout and ate the veggie. "Look at me." I chewed the broccoli loudly; little bits of green peppered the air. "I'm a goddess. Who wouldn't want me?"

Molly slowly shook her head at my self-deprecating humor.

"I don't know, Moll." I swallowed. "Ever since we danced together at that masquerade, he's always been in the back of my head, even if I didn't know who it was that I was dancing with at the time. He was supposed to be this Prince Charming that I'd never see again, and then *boom*, he shows up on his white steed to save me years later. Except...." I trailed off.

"He's kind of a dick?" Molly asked, dipping another veggie. This time she guarded it with her other hand.

"Yes! And he might not even decide to save us in the end. You know what the worst part is? He's only *kind of* a dick. He's so sweet around his daughter that...." I sighed, slumping back in my stool. There was more to Garrett Walker than what everyone knew. But it would be so much easier if there weren't.

The doorbell rang.

Molly and I shared a look. The white knight had finally arrived.

"You want me to answer?" Molly asked, crunching on her snack.

"No. I'll do it." I stood up, then took another big gulp of liquid courage. "Any last words of wisdom for me?"

"Hmm." Molly's face went sullen with concern as she weighed her thoughts. "I think you need to... use the Force."

"Okay. That's it. I hate you." I straightened out my clothes and checked the black mirror that was my phone. I showed Molly my teeth and she gave me the double thumbs-up that there weren't any broccoli stowaways.

Molly yelled for Will and Luke, then turned back and pushed me toward the door.

I took a last *last* sip of wine, exhaled and walked over.

Garrett loomed in the doorway. With his height and

winter layers on, Garrett blocked the rest of the world from view.

He'd shaved since the adventure park and, without the stubble that darkened his face, he looked a little younger and was brutally handsome. His pale blue eyes washed over me like glacial runoff. Pleased with what he saw, a faint dimple appeared in his cheek as his lips curled into a small, simple grin.

It was genuine and nice. I didn't know if it was the wine, but seeing him sent a warming calm rippling through me.

"Hi." I tucked my hair back and prayed I hadn't missed any broccoli. I did manage to hold back from smiling too big and looking like a complete fool.

"Hi, Miss Judy!" Jackie's small, adorable voice stole all the attention before Garrett could respond. She squeezed herself between us and waved.

"Hey there, Miss Jackie." I extended a hand in greeting.

"Don't take my thumb!" she cried, then spotted Will and pushed past me.

"Don't mind her. I guess they're best friends now," Garrett said in his deep, wonderful voice. His accent shined through more when he was being playful. "Unlike my daughter, I'm a vampire and need to be invited inside."

"Yes!" I stupidly swept a hand into the room. "Please come in, Count Chocula."

He greeted Molly, who'd walked over and took their coats. Garrett wore a neatly pressed charcoal gray suit without a tie and a white button-down shirt with the collar relaxed. His cologne was subtle but exotically decadent. It made me imagine us on a private beach at dusk, surrounded by a lush green forest.

"Dad's on a call with his manager," Will announced. He offered Jackie a tour of the house. Jackie looked at her father, he nodded, then off they ran.

"Ah..." Molly's mouth pulled to one side in mild annoyance. She must be no stranger to him receiving all-hour phone calls. Then she just shrugged and accepted it as she always did. "No rest for the wicked. More wine for us. Garrett?"

"Please." He accepted a glass.

"Did you find the place all right?" I asked, sitting across the bar from him.

"Turns out it's a bit of landmark. You know you're a Pokémon Go stop, right?" he asked Molly.

"Really?" I took out my phone and checked. "Ohmy-god, Molly. You totally are! How'd you find that out?"

"Wonderful," Molly groaned, obviously wanting no part of this. She sipped her drink.

"My daughter plays religiously." He shook his head in resigned acceptance, then stopped and looked up at me quizzically, a devilish expression on his face. "What level are you?"

"Twenty—" I caught my words but not the flush I felt in my face as Molly started to laugh at me. "Twenty*somethings*," I attempted to clarify, "like myself don't play kids' games, obviously."

Garrett and Molly gave me disbelieving looks, then laughed.

"Hey!" I protested, cutting my losses. Whatever. I was a nerd, *so what?* "We were all just playing video games a few hours ago. I don't want to hear it."

For the next hour or so, we talked comfortably while waiting for the roast to finish in the oven. To my surprise, Garrett asked a lot of questions about Caldwell Hope, which Molly and I answered the best we could. Working at a school, Molly was the gossip queen; she knew more of the inner workings of what was going on than I did.

For the first time since he'd been here, it finally felt like we were having a meeting. I might've been half in the bag, but it felt really productive. Garrett was curious about zoning and other technical aspects, and was soon even offering up advice for ways the stadium *could actually work.*

I dared to hope. Maybe we weren't as screwed as we thought.

Then Luke finally stepped into the room and everything fell to shit.

TWELVE
GARRETT

"You." Lucas said as he recognized me.

Lucas looked similar to how I remembered him. He wore a vintage tee and fashionably distressed jeans with no shoes. His hair was pulled back and his beard longer now than it had once been.

The fiery look in his eyes dashed my hopes that he'd have forgotten me.

"It's been awhile." I stood up to greet him and extended a hand. *Let bygones be bygones.*

He brought his hand up, but it wasn't to shake mine.

Lucas threw his weight forward and decked me. The half-full glass of wine I was holding smashed against the floor. The blow wasn't hard enough to knock me down, but I'd be feeling it for the next week or so. I exhaled, snapping my head back to guard against another strike and deliver one of my own.

Instead, I got an accusing finger pointed into my chest.

"How dare you come into my home after what you did to me in Berlin!" Lucas roared, ignoring the startled cries of Judy and Molly, who looked on in horror.

"What I did to you?" I wiped the smear of blood from the corner of my lip. I slapped his hand away and shoved him. That buried anger I felt for him bubbled to the surface. I was an idiot to think he'd changed. Guys like him were always selfish assholes. "You got what you deserved."

"My band dropped me for that!" Lucas shouted. "You opened your big fucking mouth to complain, instead of settling it with me like a man! Aaron Miller was right about you."

My eyes narrowed to slits. I was a heartbeat from putting this spoiled rock star on his ass.

"Lucas." Molly stepped between us, her sharp, dark eyes stared daggers into her husband. "The kids are here."

Sure enough, Will and Jackie stood in the hallway and watched their fathers get ready to kick the crap out of each other. The two cowered together in fear. I felt horrible. *God*, this whole night was such a mistake. I should've known better.

What the fuck was I thinking?

I quickly scooped Jackie up and reassured her that

everything was okay. To his credit Lucas did roughly the same with his son. Jackie was shaking when I picked her up. She hugged me like she thought she was never going to see me again.

As hits went, I'd taken harder. Looking down at her cherub face made me wonder how she would've dealt with seeing me get tackled by a three-hundred-pound football player. I was reminded exactly why I left the sport and was again glad I did.

"Holy crap, are you all right?" Judy asked me, rushing over.

Almost automatically she touched the side of my face. Her fingertips felt like fire on my bruised and bleeding cheek, but I didn't recoil. I didn't mind the pain. Having her that close and feeling her concern was like a warm cup of hot chocolate after being out in the cold all day.

I couldn't remember the last time anyone tried to comfort me.

"I'll get the coats." Judy glanced back at Lucas angrily, then stormed off.

He and Molly were arguing about what just happened. I didn't care as long as I could get Jackie out of here quickly. I wished she and her friend hadn't seen that.

"Are you okay, Dad?" she asked when we got to the door.

"Yeah, sweetie. Adults are just...." I couldn't find the word I was looking for.

"Adults," Jackie said, with wisdom far beyond her years.

I scoffed, seeing the truth in the innocent statement. "Yeah. Never grow up, coconut. Being an adult is overrated."

Judy came back with a pile of clothing and began handing them out. I noticed she had her own puffy coat in the pile.

"Would you mind dropping me off?" she asked with eyebrows turned up slightly. It wasn't an urgent pleading expression, but she obviously didn't want to be here anymore. "I know it's bad out there, but I don't think I'm too far out of your way."

I couldn't blame her; I sure as hell didn't want to be here either.

"Sure," I replied, helping Jackie into the last of her winter coat, gloves, scarf, and hat. "My driver, Byron, is a Marine vet. He can drive anywhere."

The snow had picked up while we were at the King residence, enough so that the ride to her place took twice as long as it would've otherwise. My limo driver was from here and assured me it wouldn't be a problem, as long as they went slow.

At some point, Jackie had fallen asleep laid out between us; she had her head on my lap and her legs on

Judy. I'd asked Judy if she minded, but she didn't. It looked like she enjoyed it even.

"You ever thought about having kids?" I asked.

"I've thought about it." Judy laughed, looking down at Jackie wistfully. "I love kids, but come on...."

"You're great with her," I said. Judy shrugged and looked out the window. *Odd.* Was that a sore subject? "I understand kids aren't for everyone. Hell they *definitely* weren't for me back in my MVP days."

"What changed?" Judy asked distantly, gazing at the heavy snowfall through the tinted windows.

"Fate, I guess." Fate was also cruel. *It gives and it takes away.*

For a few minutes we sat in silence and the lights automatically dimmed into a low, cool driving hue. I pushed away thoughts of Heidi.

Judy battled whatever was going on in her own head. I wished I knew her better. I wanted to remove some of the anguish that was plainly written across her face.

Five years ago, Judy danced into my life so briefly at the exact wrong time, and now again at the exact wrong time we had these three *not*-dates before we parted ways forever. It was almost déjà vu, but so much worse.

We we're reliving a moment that never happened.

"What happened in Germany?" Judy asked abruptly. "I mean, I know the story, the one on the news at least. Luke naked and drugged out of his mind, crashed through all the band equipment during a show. But…" She turned to face me. The soft blue lighting in the accents, doors and ceiling cast her in an ethereal glow. "What role did you play?"

It looked like she was made of stardust.

Beautiful.

"Why did he deck me, you mean?" I glanced at her. The dull pain throbbed like it was taking a nap and woke up by me mentioning it.

"That. Yeah." She cringed at what I might say. Her face crinkled up as if it were sore too.

"The reason Lucas was naked was because he was fucking my date during the band's instrumental solos." I said the words flatly. I barely remembered the girl now, but I was fuming back then. At the time, I was angrier that he made me look like a chump than I was upset about my date.

I was such a different person now, that it felt like it happened to someone else.

"Really?" Judy was all wide-eyed and jaw agape. She couldn't believe it. "How did you not kill Luke for that? I'd have been pissed."

"I was there for the all-star games that year. I was going to beat the shit out of him, but he was already such a mess on drugs that it wouldn't have been satisfying. I told the tourism committee that one of us was leaving in a body bag if they didn't get him the fuck out of Berlin.

They ended up banning his whole band from playing anywhere in that city."

"*That's* why his band dropped him." Judy pushed her air out, as if finally putting some puzzle pieces together in her head.

"I guess." Once I flew back home, I buried myself in pussy and football until I eventually met my wife. I kept that part to myself, not because I was ashamed of any of it, it just led to... dark places that I didn't want to think or talk about.

"He never actually told me the whole story," Judy mused.

"Probably because it made him look like an asshole," I replied. Jackie stirred on my lap, so I brushed down her hair until she settled again.

"What was he talking about? Who's Aaron Miller? Luke mentioned him earlier. My dad actually mentioned him to me, too, right before you jumped out of your helicopter."

Fucking Aaron Miller.

I rubbed my forehead. "He was my coach. This short, angry man with a sadistic chip on his shoulder. He felt that I owed all my success to him because he originally scouted me. I broke my contract and retired right before the championship game that would've made him statistically one of the best coaches of all time. They lost because of it and the history books passed him by. To put it nicely, we didn't get along."

We fucking hated *each other.*

"Oh yeah!" Judy lit up. "I saw his interview on *Oprah*. Well, part of it. I turned it off when he went on and on about you diluting the 'integrity of the game'."

"That whole thing was part of his retaliation against me." I exhaled darkly. That was right after the accident. That fucking asshole.

That was a long time ago, I reminded myself. I took a deep breath and changed the subject to something less infuriating. "Why can't the King family fund the stadium? Their net worth has only risen since Richard took over all facets of the family business."

"They didn't want it built in the first place." Judy shrugged

I chuckled and muttered, "Of all the things to agree with them on... but still, Caldwell Hope is synonymous with *that* family."

"It's... a long story. But due to some crazy shenanigans that brought the brothers back together, they're kind of broke now. I mean by billionaire standards," Judy clarified. "Gloria explained it once to me and it made my head spin."

The car slowed to a stop just outside Judy's condo.

"This is me." She scooched as carefully as possible, trying to prevent Jackie from waking up. Jackie flopped over gracelessly and did her best sleeping starfish impression.

"It's slippery out there." I prevented my daughter from falling off the seat, then laid her down more comfortably. I grabbed a small blanket to cover her, then stepped out of the car. "I'll walk you out."

"Oh, you don't have to," Judy said, carefully walking around the back of the limo to the walkway. Then she fell.

I reached out, snapped my arms around her shoulders and just barely caught her. I was surprised that I didn't topple over with her.

"You were saying?" I asked, looking down at her.

"I'm okay." Her feet kicked out and slid against the ice-covered walkway, then eventually found their footing. "You're fast. How'd you even do that?"

"I'm good with my hands." I held her a little longer than was necessary before letting her go. It felt nice to have her in my arms.

"I'm sorry about dinner," she said when we reached her door.

"You didn't know." I put an arm against the wall for extra support. I couldn't believe how icy everything was. Someone could get really hurt. Who was supposed to maintain this area?

Judy unlocked and opened the door slowly. Despite what happened at the King's house, I didn't want the night to end just yet. Time slowed when she turned to face me; her green eyes shone brightly in the dim light. Red, from the cold, touched her cheeks. The air quietly crackled between us. I felt like a high schooler bringing his date home.

Had I ever had this moment? I wondered. Even back then I'd never been on traditional dates. Between studying and football practice, I never had the time.

"I had a lot of fun kicking your ass in video games earlier." Her lips spread mischievously; the winter chill robbed them of their rosy glow. The snow had tapered off. Residual flakes were swept up in the cutting breeze. Judy recoiled against a burst that peppered the side of her face.

"What did Molly whisper to you at the arcade?" I pulled my glove off and thumbed the cold white specks from her cheeks.

"She said that you were the best kind of trouble and warned me to be careful." She opened her eyes and stared into mine.

"That's at least two warnings now." I slid my hand into the back of her hood and pulled her closer. "Do you think she's right?"

"I think you're a lot of things." Judy closed her eyes again and allowed herself to feel my hot breath on her lips. Her words became nearly inaudible. They were meant only for me. "Trouble is definitely one of them."

Her lips were tinged with cold, but beyond that, she was fire and lust. She all but fell into me as the brief peck I gave her turned into something more. I took my time with her, tasting and feeling her mouth with my own. Every flick of our tongues was magic, and lights, and warmth.

I wanted to stay in that moment until the sun burned out of the sky.

"Dad?" Jackie asked loudly through a crack in the window.

All good things..., I thought, with no small degree of disappointment. Our lips parted with a small pop. Judy lurched forward a few inches, not wanting the kiss to end either. Being a parent was the best thing that ever happened to me, but Goddamn if it wasn't inconvenient now and then.

"Mr. Walker... I—" Judy gasped in breath, as if she'd only now remembered that she needed air to survive.

"Call me Garrett." I smiled at her, then turned back toward the limo and my daughter.

I sipped my coffee and gazed into the spitting, crackling fire oblivious to the families and couples that wandered around me. The Twin Pines lodge at the base of Beaverkill Mountain thrummed with activity, but I was too lost in the kiss from last night to notice any of it.

Call me Garrett.

Those three words echoed in my mind and heart as I stared into the dancing flame of the central hearth.

My mind had been drifting all last night while I painted and throughout the day today. I was beyond useless at work. Monica sent me home after grilling me on every detail about my meetings with Garrett. I told her everything.

Everything but the kiss.

That was mine.

Two young lovers came in from a long day's worth of

skiing. Their infatuation was so strong that it was impossible not to notice them. They'd removed their bulky coats and snuggled up together on the long bench near me. Whispered words, stolen breaths, and countless kisses passed between them.

Watching them was like stepping into a time machine. They were a glimpse at what *we* could've been, had our lives been different when we met. Could Garrett and I have had this?

A wave of sadness rolled over me at the sight of such exuberant love. They didn't have a care in the world, other than themselves. How nice that must feel.

What am I doing?

I looked back at the fire feeling stupid. Stupid for dreaming. There was no future for us. There wasn't even a present. I was here to sell him a deal, and he was obligated to listen to me for one more day.

It didn't mean anything. It was just a kiss—a warm, soft, exploratory kiss that ended far too soon.

My mind started drifting again to seeing him in the gym. It made my body ache to be crushed beneath him. I could still feel his big, strong hands close over my shoulders from when he caught me last night.

A shiver rocked me, from between my shoulder blades straight down to my inner thighs. Just the thought of him began to get me wet. I had to start carrying an extra pair of underwear in my purse if I knew I was going to see him.

How could one man be so sexy?

"Hi." The crisp, deep voice from behind the long bench spoke into my ear.

"Jesus!" I startled in my seat, and pressed a hand to my chest. Was I thinking about him so hard that I actually summoned him? I wished I went to Hogwarts so I could learn that spell.

"I've never been called that before," Garrett said carelessly as he rounded the bench. He pointed downward. "Typically they associate me with the other guy. I hope I didn't keep you waiting too long."

"No," I said, trying to calm myself. *Fuck, his voice was hot.*

Garrett wore black-and-red snow pants and a coat. Even the bulkier winter clothing looked neatly tailored to him. It fit snug but was still loose enough to move. He also wore a face mask that was pulled down to the chin and goggles that were slid up over his eyebrows.

Was he planning on skiing? I thought we were here to talk with management and go over their numbers. This was part of his "community gauging". He wanted to see how the other big tourist attraction in the area was doing.

"I think we'd better hurry though." I straightened myself. I wasn't kitted up like he was. All I had on was boots, pants, a blouse—with a bust line a little lower than what was work appropriate—and a cardigan. "I think the mountain is closing up early today. I thought it was from the blizzard they say is on the way, but now I'm not so sure. I think there might be some sort of special event going on tonight."

"We'd better hurry then." Garrett replaced the goggles and face mask with a low-slung baseball cap.

It wasn't until we reached the executive elevators, and after he was stopped by some bubbling fans, that I realized why he wore the ski gear. It was for anonymity. *Duh!*

Garrett Walker was handsome, powerful, sexy beyond belief, and amazing at everything. But by being so close to him these last few days, it was easy to forget that he was also a celebrity. A big one, too.

It wasn't just that he was a football hero. He'd been in movies, and had cameos in music videos. In his prime, before he stepped away from it all, he had been an A-list public figure. Everyone knew his name and face.

Garrett politely signed a few autographs, which included a little boy's shirt, then took a selfie with the kid's mom. Soon the few people that surrounded him became a small mob, all of them wanting his picture and signature. Fortunately the elevator doors opened before we were completely overwhelmed.

I immediately felt claustrophobic. I liked people, but

this was quickly becoming too much. It was all so aggressive. How did he deal with that everywhere he went?

"Does that ever get old? The whole *being famous* thing? I can't imagine what it's like to have everyone know me wherever I go."

"It's something I had to accept a long time ago." Garrett shrugged easily, then after a short time he added, "It does bother me a little when I'm with my daughter. I've sold myself to the public, but they have no right over her."

Garrett's expression darkened a little.

I opened my mouth to comment, but thought better of it. *It must be hard to know that strangers were taking pictures of your little girl and saying whatever they wanted about her in the press.* It wasn't my place to talk about that sort of thing with him.

I was still basically a stranger to him too.

"Did you have someone clear my walkway?" I asked half-jokingly, wanting to lighten the mood a bit.

"No, of course not." He scoffed at the absurd notion. He was a billionaire, that sort of thing was extremely beneath him. The doors chirped, then opened onto a landing before a floor lined with cubicles. A young man in a polo and khakis was armed with a broad smile and waited patiently for us. Garrett held the elevator doors open for me to exit first. "I did it myself."

"Yeah, I didn't think so. I just thought it was weird

that—" I mindlessly walked out, then stopped and jerked my head back toward Garrett in disbelief. "Wait, what?

My overactive imagination pictured him out front of my condo tossing heaping shovelfuls of snow to either side of my walk way. In my head, he was naked to the waist, and the windswept snow that struck him steamed off his corded muscles.

"I wanted to make sure it was done right. I couldn't risk you slipping and breaking your neck before our last... meeting." Garrett stepped past me and shook the hand of the man waiting for us.

I couldn't help but smile when no one was looking at me. That couldn't have been the real reason. Could it? Gah! Garrett was so frustrating. The second I thought I had him figured, he threw me a curveball.

We were soon joined by the resort's owner and his wife. They took us on a tour of the facility and answered all of Garrett's questions. Garrett's customary surgical precision came across in the conversation. He quickly put the owner back on his heels.

Everyone scrambled to accommodate the Grim Reaper of Wall Street any way they could. When Garrett turned on his corporate tone, he was downright terrifying. Sharp and thorough, he could slice right through people to get to the truth. I wondered if anyone could hide anything from him.

And God help the poor fool that gets in his way.

Garrett eventually got what he needed from the shaken couple and ended the meeting curtly. He wasn't impressed and he let them know that, but ever the professional, he thanked them for their time.

Honestly, I was a little surprised by the ski resort's lack of certain safety precautions. They were staggeringly understaffed for what they needed. It wasn't my problem, so I tried to put it out of my mind. I had enough on my plate. By the time we got back into the lodge, the sun was just about to set and all of the guests, tourists, and customers had all left.

The mountain was now closed.

"Care for a drink?" Garrett asked, making his way to a nearby bartender in an adjacent room.

"Here?" I asked. "I think they're closing."

"That wasn't what I asked." Garrett turned away and nodded to the bartender. He ordered two glasses of wine.

I slowly made my way toward him as I glanced around. An employee put another log on the fire, then began tidying the area up and tending it. Behind him, I saw the ski shop and cafeteria were still open. All the staff was present in fact. Through the big windows I could see that the mountain itself was lit and the ski lifts were all on.

They only thing that was different was the lack of patrons.

So they weren't closing. It must be a private function then. Either way we'd still have to leave.

Garrett tipped the man, then handed me a glass. "Have you ever been night skiing?"

"No." I took the glass, then glanced around again. No one rushed over asking us to leave. It started to dawn on me. "Is this you? Did you rent the entire mountain for us?"

"I've always wanted to. Night riding is on my short list." Garrett ignored my question and took a sip of his wine. "I've just never got around to it. Have you ever tried it?"

"Once. In college." I'd worked at a resort like this briefly. I'd seen private functions, birthday parties, and wedding receptions being held in certain halls here of course, but the whole mountain.... I'd never even heard of someone doing this before.

Holy crap! How much did something like that cost? Hundreds of thousands? *Millions?*

Who spends that kind of money on a whim?

Garrett. *That's who.*

"Great, I need a guide." Garrett downed the rest of his glass, then waved someone over.

"I don't have any of my gear." I set my glass of barely touched wine on the counter.

"That's fine." Garrett cocked his head toward the ski shop. "Let's get you some."

Garrett refused my feeble attempts at protesting. Despite what I said, I loved the mini shopping spree.

I got to try on all the gear I'd always wanted but could never justify. There was state-of-the-art antifogging goggles; Bluetooth-enabled helmet with built in speakers; sweat-wicking thermals with interwoven smart fabric that regulated body temperature; GPS-impregnated ski jacket with hard pads sewn into the cinched-up lining. The list went on.

After an hour of playing dress up, we finally hit the slopes. All the lifts were running. We had free range over the whole mountain. It was still hard to wrap my head around. It was so surreal that it felt like I was swimming through a dream.

"So, Garrett, is this what billionaires do to impress girls?" I slid my skis and poles into the square bin at the front of the gondola, then stepped inside.

"Only if it's working." Garrett wore an easy grin. He followed suit and slid his snowboard in the square bin as well.

I was able to use his first name and even get a smile from him occasionally. Had he really changed that much in the last three days?

I thought about the way he interacted with the resort owners and the staff, and realized I was wrong. He was still stern and cold around most people, but not me. Butterflies swarmed in my stomach as the gondola abruptly took off. I wobbled, but Garrett quickly steadied me. He lent me a hand to help me sit down as the great enclosed basket swung on the thick steel cable and began its climb up the mountain.

That fluttering I felt had nothing to do with the gondola, I realized. *He's let me in.* I felt special and a little worried. Garrett was a notorious playboy. How much of this was truly for me?

"You know this still isn't a date, right?" Jealously washed over me. It twisted my gut into a sailor's knot. I tried to harden myself to it. Tomorrow, Garrett might be out of my life altogether. "We're just two people sharing a fun winter hobby."

I hated the idea of being won over by money being thrown around near me, but I loved to ski. Nearly everyone went their whole life without ever getting an experience like this. The whole mountain to ourselves.... It was unthinkable.

"Not a date, huh? What scares you more?" Garrett asked, staring into my eyes. He leaned closer to me so that he was all I saw. His scent, the sound of his voice, the heat that emanated off him.... Garrett invaded my senses one by one in that lonely gondola on that empty mountain. He and I were the only two people in the universe at that moment. "That I might be interested in you, or that I might not be?"

I swallowed hard.

"What makes you think *I'm* interested in *you?*" It sounded ridiculous even before I got all the words out. Of course I wanted him. I've wanted him since the Halloween party so long ago, back before I even knew who he was.

"A boy can dream." Garrett winked at me, then began to bundle back up as the high-speed gondola slowed to a stop at the top of the mountain.

I pulled my new mask up across my face just before a smile erupted across my face. It should be criminal to be that smooth. He should be locked away in some sort of jail for being too sexy, where regular girls like me can't get to him.

I was flying too close to the sun and my wax wings were beginning to melt, but what a glorious way to go.

I PULLED THE NEOPRENE BANDANNA DOWN TO MY chin, closed my eyes, and filled my lungs with pure mountain air. Steam escaped me. I did it again. Of all my dangerous vices, I didn't realize how much I missed snowboarding until I felt the crunch of graded snow beneath my feet.

The elated feeling of freedom was intoxicating.

I looked over at Judy. She was wrapped in the pink hues of light dying miles behind her. Here on the mountaintop, the sunlight hadn't completely faded. She had already strapped herself in and was waiting patiently for me to do the same.

The view was magnificent. *She* was magnificent.

It actually pained me to look at her, especially after that kiss last night. The phantom taste of her lips echoed across my tongue all day. I'd waited half a decade to do that, and it was every bit worth the wait.

This was the last night of the three days I promised her. Our commitment was over. It all felt too sudden, but it was necessary. For Jackie's sake, I needed to break whatever Judy and I had off before my daughter got hurt.

"You ready?" I yelled over the screaming wind, after snapping into my bindings.

"I'm waiting on you, old man," she shot back, then planted both poles and thrust herself forward past me.

Old man? I scoffed, hopping forward on my board, then cutting in after her. *So she wants to play a game?*

I got low and flew down the trails after her. We stayed only on the ones that were lit with the massive flood lights. Everything else was too dark even for me. Judy was good, *real good*, but I was still faster. My back leg carved tight, fast grooves in the snow and soon enough I became her shadow.

"Tag," I shouted, slapping her square on the ass as I passed by.

Her head cocked around so abruptly that I thought she might fall. Worried, I slowed down to make sure she was alright. The fox played me like a flute, capitalizing on my compassion to blow by me. She tagged my shoulder as she passed.

Trail after trail, I led most of the game, taking unfair advantages where I could. She was great on the open trails, probably a little better than I was even, but I excelled everywhere she was afraid to go. Occasionally, I'd slip into the trees and do some night forest riding—always staying close enough to the edge of the trail to use lit sections of woods—or I'd take her through the parks and soar over her head on some of the bigger jumps.

We played that way for hours as the snow fell faster and wetter. If Judy minded, she didn't show it. I told the owners to send most of the staff home including the lifties. We'd only be riding the gondola and that was completely automated. There was no reason to make lift attendants suffer unnecessarily for our childish games.

Both of us knew what it was like to endure cold, shitty days. It turned out that each of us had worked for a season at a ski resort when we were younger—her during a break in university, and me just after school before football training camp. On the gondola up, we shared a flask of whiskey I kept in my pocket and shared war stories from the times we worked on the mountain.

"No way! You did not seriously spray paint his car." Judy roared incredulously between fits of laughing.

"It was his own damn fault. Our landlord had us living virtually on top of one another. You get that many drunken mountain rats partying in the same house for two months and...." I smiled, remembering a half dozen other equally crazy stories. I took a long pull of the flask and continued. "Well, let's just say, that wasn't the worst of it. It was a real shame, too. The place was gorgeous before we arrived. Three floors, game room, fully stocked bar, two entertainment centers, and Jacuzzi on the patio."

"Sounds like nineteen-year-old Garrett was in heaven." Judy's eyes twinkled as she looked at me. It wasn't hard to see the admiration there. It was an incredible feeling. I wasn't famous in her eyes. I was *special.*

She was my dancing partner again—someone to share in a grand adventure with. I'd done so much by myself, but with her, I felt as if I was getting the whole experience. I got to see the excitement in her eyes and knew that we went through it together. I could see myself plainly in her brilliant green eyes and it warmed me more than the whiskey.

Dangerous, a small careful voice said deep within me. I tried to push it away but, it lingered, growing only louder. *Don't fall for her. You know it can never work, especially not after what you're about to do to her.*

"Garrett?" Judy repeated, snatching the flask away. "Are you in still there? Us American girls aren't that boring, I hope."

"No, of course not. Sorry. My mind ran away from me for a moment." I snapped out of the ominous thoughts and regarded her fully again. "What was that?"

"I *said*—" She gave me a playful sidelong look while

taking a sip from the flask then continued, "—was that your first time in the States?"

"Yeah. Then football took over." I chuckled. "Apparently I couldn't keep away from your country after that."

"Dad played football briefly in college."

"Yeah?" It would make sense why he held on so tightly to the stadium, despite not being the best choice to run it. "Was he any good?"

"He was all right, I guess." She shrugged noncommittally. "I think he'd have been better suited to be a ref instead, honestly. He knows everything there is to know."

I tucked that bit of info into the back of my mind. I could picture Paul as a referee. "I can tell you're not much of a sports fan, are you?"

"Oh, yeah?" she replied with a sassy shake of shoulders that was adorable. "And what do sports fans look—"

The entire mountain abruptly closed its eyes on us.

In huge chunks, all the lights went out on the mountain, including our gondola which whirred to a lazy stop high above the trail. Judy screamed and we pitched to the side as the wind picked up and forced our little cabin into a heavy swing.

"It'll be all right." I grabbed her tightly. Whatever happened I wouldn't let her out of my arms.

Without the whir of the engine and soft music playing, the whipping, driving wind smashing against our hanging carriage was uncomfortably loud. If turbulence were a sound, it would be a lot like this.

Red emergency lights flicked on, first at the lodge far below, then at each lift including ours. The gondola engine winded up and at about half speed, ambled on toward the top of the mountain. We were just over one pole away from the drop off point. If we could only make it....

In the red light, the blizzard we'd been ignoring took on a demonic presence. The regular white trail lights couldn't catch just how hard it was snowing. The sky was a falling red haze that looked more akin to fire than ice.

Then again, the winter swallowed that too. The backup power cracked off with a loud, frightening pop.

"Fuck!" Judy cried, as another gust took hold and rattled us in what was quickly becoming an oversize coffin.

This light fun time just took a hard turn. My instincts turned with it. A surging need to protect this woman in my arms took over. The only thing that mattered was getting Judy to safety.

When the wind settled down, I realized that the conditions were too dangerous for them to send anyone up for us and with the heat off in the gondola, we wouldn't last the night without freezing to death, despite our fantastic gear.

We needed to get off this thing ourselves.

"I-I can't. NO fucking way." Judy lowered her head. She'd begun shaking when I explained my plan. The carriage swung in defiance, as if reinforcing the idea that she wasn't going to make it.

"Judy." I stripped off my gloves and took her face in my hands. "I promise that I will keep you safe."

She wasn't convinced; fear had overcome her. I needed to get her to safety, and to do that I had to connect with her.

The wind howled and smashed against us again, which caused the suspension cord that held us aloft to start creaking. I knew it wasn't going to snap, but it certainly sounded like it might.

"You owe me," I said gruffly. She finally looked up at me, confused. "On that dance hall floor I saved your life. Now I need you to save mine. I won't leave here without you, so the only way I'm ever getting down is if you're safely with me. Do you understand?" I waited a beat and then repeated. "You owe me."

She just swallowed and stared at me for a long breath, then eventually nodded. I kissed her on the forehead for reassurance.

I pulled the emergency release lever on the sliding doors and opened us to a blast of arctic cold. Fortunately, the extra backup power—as brief as it was—got the gondola to within easy reach of the suspension pole. We were way too high to jump out safely, but at least we had a way down.

The rest was agonizingly slow going. I went out first, testing my grip and the foot rungs. Satisfied, I waved her over. It was a one-man ladder; two people on it at the same time was dangerous and uncomfortable, but I stayed close in case she needed me.

Judy was on the inside center of the rungs, and I wrapped myself around her like a security blanket. We descended, one rung at a time, until we hit the trail fifty feet below. Our gear was out in front of the gondola and getting to it was impossible. Even if we did, the trails were nearly pitch black. Traversing them without a light would be fatal.

I took Judy's hand and we started the arduous climb *up* the mountain.

The roofed drop off point for the gondola was high enough that the faint remaining natural light silhouetted it. I trudged a path for us through knee-high snow until we reached it.

This wouldn't be a good shelter, I decided, taking a long look around. Typically the gondolas came up, slowed to a crawl around a wide rotary, people exited, grabbed their gear, then the gondolas sped up again and made the return trip down the mountain. This building was basically a gazebo with an enclosed maintenance room. No, we'd have to make it to the satellite lodge near the actual peak of the mountain.

That meant more hiking.

We rested for a time. I checked Judy for signs of hypothermia or frostbite, but the gear she had on held up to the price tag. When she'd caught her breath, we began the trek further up the mountain. This time it was much more difficult. Not only was it nearly three times longer of a walk, but pushing through the now waist-high snow was like walking through cold, loose sand.

It took us nearly an hour, but we made it up to the small lodge. All the doors were locked, save the kitchen entrance. It was completely dark inside. Although I had no reception, my watch had a fairly bright flashlight app. It wasn't the best, but it helped me navigate the small rooms.

The lodge was a tenth the size of the one at the bottom of the mountain but was laid out in a similar way. There was a main entrance with a fireplace, which was a staple for every ski resort I'd ever been in. I'd never understood the concept—the lodges were always warm enough for me without it, but I read something some-where about a crackling flame having a calming effect on people.

Instead of a restaurant and bar, there was a cafe, instead of a merch shop, there were a few racks of smaller portable items. There was of course a ski repair shop, but it only dealt in minor stuff like loose bindings and board and ski waxing.

Judy was exhausted. She tripped over a chair in the main hall. Gloved hands slid down my jacket groping for purchase but finding none. When I turned around, she was already on the floor.

"Leave me. I'm a goner," she said between breathless

pants. She wore an exhausted but not pained expression on her face. She was so heavily padded with skiing gear and snow that I doubted she even felt the impact. She tried to get up, then just laid on the floor and sprawled out.

"There's no hope for me," she continued on dramatically. "I'll only slow you down. Let my epitaph read *Judy Sullivan, world renowned player of video games and beater of Garrett Walker at racing.*"

Even with the heat completely off, the lodge itself was still warm from a full day's use. It would eventually get cold, but we'd survive, especially if I found the split logs they were using for the main fireplace.

"Should I have them carve *delusional* above or below your name on the headstone?" I laid on the long bench above her and let my arm fall to the floor. The light from my watch brightened our whole section. "You didn't win."

"Yes, I did."

I craned my neck over to look at her. "For someone who was nearly hyperventilating with fear earlier, you're surprisingly chipper."

"You promised to keep me safe," Judy said sweetly enough to make my heart skip a beat.

"You fell for that?"

"Jerk." She slapped my arm.

I recoiled playfully but otherwise stayed silent. I was exhausted, too. Between contacting the authorities, the resort management, my company, and making sure we could get rescued soon, there was still so much to do. I just needed a few minutes to rest first.

"Thank you." Judy took my gloved hand in her own and squeezed. I didn't respond. I didn't need to. I was telling the truth earlier. I'd protect her with everything I had. It gave me an overwhelming sensation of purpose.

If I could save her, maybe she could save me....

I pushed the silly thought away, and for a while, we rested and basked in being alive.

"What do you think happened?" she asked.

"No idea. Some sort of critical failure, I'd guess." I took off my gloves and unzipped my jacket; a plume of steam escaped. I was sweating like crazy from the hike. "Whatever it was, it had to be bad. I'll go look for a walkie in a minute."

"What if it's the zombie apocalypse?" Judy sounded so serious that I almost considered it. Then her lips curled, telling me she was joking.

"Unless zombies can drive snowmobiles, I figure we got a shot at making it through the night."

My watch alarm vibrated curtly. It was 8:00 p.m.

Shit.

I shot up and immediately began looking for offices.

"What's wrong now?" Judy called after me, hints of

worry creeping back into her voice. I told her to wait there for me. I had exactly one hour to get us rescued.

Funny, I thought sardonically.

In keeping one promise with Judy, I might end up breaking another. And not just a regular promise... the most important one I'd ever made.

When Garrett eventually returned, he looked more defeated than I'd ever seen him. A look of curious surprise at the crackling fire diluted that a bit. He had towels draped over one shoulder and was holding a walkie-talkie.

"You got the fire going?" he asked.

"Yeah," I declared proudly. "Apparently this coat comes with a flashlight, fire starter, and some other goodies. It's a regular end-of-the-world-with-Garrett-Walker emergency survival kit."

The temperature in the small lodge dropped considerably in the time he was gone. The fire helped, but the room was too big for all of it to be heated. I'd hung up my jacket and snow pants on the back of a chair to dry. I still wore my thermals, but they were cold, wet, and gross with sweat from the climb.

"You're going to need to change out of those wet clothes," Garrett said solemnly and handed me a towel. "We can wash the thermals in a kitchen sink. Once they're dry, we can put them back on. Until then, we run the risk of frostbite."

His cold corporate tone edged back into his voice.

"What's going on?" I asked. After all we'd been through, I finally got the Garrett I'd met at the masquerade ball back. I didn't want to lose that version of him, especially if we were trapped in an ice fortress together.

"We're not getting rescued tonight." He sat down on the bench closest to the fire and took off his boots. He rubbed the weariness out of his face and dragged both hands back through his hair. "Freak lightning bolt struck the lodge and caused a fire. All the emergency helicopters are busy. Hell, mine was even requisitioned by the fire department for additional aide."

"So?" I asked. "It's just one night. It might be uncomfortable, but it wasn't like we were freezing to death on the gondola. There should be enough firewood to get us through the night. If not we can burn some of the wooden benches. We should be alright I think, right?"

"It's not that—" Garrett's watch vibrated and lit up again. It was another alarm like the one that got him moving so quickly an hour ago. He tore it off and whipped it against the wall. I flinched from the sharp crack of the glass screen busting apart. "It's something else."

Garrett went quiet for a while, just staring into the fire.

"Then what is it?" Some people could pull off brooding and simmering anger, like Luke for instance, but Garrett couldn't. He was too cocksure and confident by nature. This darkness behind his face and posture made him look unsettling.

"I'd rather not talk about it," he said definitively.

I sighed, realizing I wasn't going to reach him. At least not like this. I clicked on my flashlight and padded into the kitchen with the towel to change out of my thermals. The air had a definite chill, but the rubber pad by the sinks at least kept the floor from freezing my feet.

I stripped down, wrapped myself in the towel and let my clothes soak. There was still some warm water so I washed up as best I could in the second sink. It wasn't great, but I felt much less gross.

Leaning ungracefully on the counter, I rattled something small on the attached shelf. In my mind, standing there all alone in the relative dark, the thing that moved was a ball of spiders jumping out to attack me. I nearly shrieked. Then I realized spiders didn't wear armor, and what fell was made of some kind of metal. It bounced off the shelf, rolled down the length of the counter before dropping to the floor.

Shining the flashlight on it, I saw that it was a portable metal burner, the kind you use for parties when you want to keep a tray of food warm while people served themselves. Did they really have functions up here too?

Then I had a brilliant idea.

A short while later, I walked back into the room with the fireplace. Garrett had his shirt off and was cleaning his arms, chest, and face with baby wipes he'd probably found in the small baby-changing station near the bathrooms.

The firelight licked over his body, making every sculpted contour more dramatic. Deep shadowed ridges ran along his flexing triceps and between his cut chest and abs. The light was too afraid to show all of him to me, in case I exploded. When my eyes drank in the hard V lines that started above his hips and disappeared into his form-fitted long johns, I felt my stomach tighten.

I took a step back and lingered in the doorway to watch him. Watching him like that felt scandalous, but I couldn't help myself. He moved with such strength and smoothness as he finished with the baby wipes and began to stretch sore muscles.

As an artist, I wanted to paint him, capture his raw, masculine power. As a red-blooded woman, I wanted to jump him and let him have his way with me.

"You're a bit of a voyeur, aren't you?"

"What? No!" I startled, clearing my throat. "I'm, uh, meditating. Near-death experience and all that."

"I'm sorry to hear you were in such danger before you snuck into the gym yesterday." Garrett raised an eyebrow; the hint of a smirk creased his lips. He'd calmed down a little while I was away.

"I brought you something." I cleared my dry throat again, quickly changing the subject. I was glad for the darkness, then maybe he wouldn't see me blush so fiercely. "Figured it might cheer you up. It always did the trick for me when I was in a bad mood."

Garrett eyed the two mugs in my hands as I walked over. Then his eyes caught hold of everything that wasn't covered by my towel. My bare shoulders, neck, and cleavage tingled beneath his steamy stare.

"Here. Hot chocolate." I handed the warm mug to him. I hated that I wanted him to like what he saw. I sat down beside him on the bench. "Well, not *hot*. More like lukewarm chocolate unfortunately."

Garrett chuckled and stared into the dark drink. "First time I ever had this was my second week working at Mt. Snow in Vermont." He took a sip then glanced over to me, his icy demeanor thawed considerably. "Thanks."

"I'm a firm believer in chocolate therapy." I dragged a shy smile to the corner of my mouth. "Chocolate and wine." I turned to face him fully and asked, "Is everything all right?"

Garrett took a deep breath.

"Jackie's second birthday..." His tone bordered on somber. The firelight danced and flickered in his pupils. "...we'd just crushed New Orleans. It was a home game: matinée show. I was at the stadium having a beer with some of the tailgaters and signing ball caps in the parking lot. Not something I did often, but I was in a great mood that day, so I figured what the hell?

"Heidi and I had mostly patched things up and were going to try and make it work, for Jackie's sake. She was driving in with our daughter. I had the whole night planned." Garrett smiled, remembering.

His smile evaporated.

"I got the news in the locker room after my shower," he said. "There'd been an accident. You probably heard about it in the news a while back."

I nodded.

Gloria's news about what happened to his wife sprang freshly into my mind. This was an extremely intimate story he was sharing with me. I felt honored, but a little unworthy, to hear it. I didn't know Garrett all that well.

Why tell a virtual stranger something this personal?

"It was a miracle that Jackie survived it." His gaze

never strayed from the fire. "What the news didn't say was what they found in the car that hit my wife."

"Some beer bottles?" I guessed.

"Signed ball cap," he said. "I'd been drinking with one of the bastard's who went on to murder my wife."

"Jesus...." It was so much worse than I originally thought. After what he'd been through, it was no wonder he was a hardened jerk sometimes.

"If I hadn't—" His voice choked off. "I wanted to bring us together. I ended up doing the opposite. I made a promise to Jackie when Heidi died. I told her that until she outgrew me, I would always be home to kiss her goodnight." He paused; the weight of the promise wore heavily on him. "Tonight, I became a liar."

Wow, I thought. *Every night?*

"There's nothing you could've done." I gently touched his knee. "It was a freak accident."

"There's always something I could've done," Garrett said gravely and let the issue rest.

"Why are you telling me this?"

"I don't know." He looked at me, his defined features lit starkly by the fire. "I guess I just needed to finally tell someone."

And tonight's our last night together. I won't be around to remind you of what you told me.

"There's a freedom in telling a secret to a stranger." He leaned in, his hot breath brushing my cheek and ear.

And he kissed me.

"W ait." G arrett tore his lips from mine, which left me gasping. The torrent of kisses had come on so suddenly and so passionately that I fell completely into them. I was making out with a dream.

"I don't have a condom," he said through gritted teeth. "The one time I didn't bring one...."

"I'm insulted." I smirked, feeling the wave of lust crash inside me. And like a drug addict beginning the painful descent into withdrawal, my body began to switch gears. I was ready for him. I wanted it so bad it hurt, and to deny myself that was just so cruel.

"Don't be." He adjusted the bulge in his long thermal underpants. I could barely keep my eyes from widening at how big it had become since we'd started kissing. "I'm not that virtuous. I've had one in my pocket since the morning I picked you up at your condo. It had your name all over it."

"Are you clean?" I asked, a little more sheepishly than I'd meant to. "I mean not literally. I know we just hiked forever and a day, so of course you're probably a little sweaty still. I mean STDs. You don't have any, right?"

"Fuck no. I have a daughter. I make sure to get checked every month, despite always wearing a condom. She's not going to get rid of me that easily." Garrett winked at the dark humor.

"It's fine then," I said, mustering up the courage to get out the next part. I probably wouldn't have been able to say it if he hadn't shared that private piece of his life with me a few minutes ago. It also didn't help that I was hornier than I'd ever been in my whole life. "I— I can't have kids." I paused. He could tell I didn't want to talk about it and didn't press me for any details. "Oh and yeah, I'm clean, too."

Garrett touched my face, drawing me closer to him. He had a way of melting my brain to soup. Whenever I day dreamed, it was always about how he would touch me in this moment if it ever happened.

Garrett threw his opened coat on the carpet in front of the fireplace and positioned me on it.

Garrett didn't look like a football player, not really. Up close, with all his scars and tattoos, he looked more like a martial artist. His body was unbelievable. He was a ripped mountain of sex, masquerading as a man. I wanted to paint all his hard ridges... with my tongue.

Garrett was gentler with me than I thought he would be. There were so many layers to him, it was insane. I couldn't help but think of the way he treated his daughter. You'd never know his capacity for kindness and generosity by the way the media portrays him.

He did that on purpose. His daughter only saw the loving father. Garrett was the Grim Reaper everywhere, except where it mattered to him most. The fact that I was allowed to see that side of him gave me goose bumps.

Even as he kissed my neck and dragged his fingers through my scalp, I felt the tiniest bit self-conscious. Should I have told him that? Only Gloria knew about my miscarriage and the damaging results with Doug.

"Stop it," Garrett said gruffly.

"Stop what? I'm not doing anything," I replied innocently. Did I say anything out loud? No, I kept that hard secret to myself. He couldn't read my mind, could he? Of course not. He was a billionaire, not a superhero.

"You're getting tense. Here and—" His strong hands massaged my shoulders right above my collarbones.

I moaned, my muscles becoming puddles,

"Here," he finished, working his hands up the side and back of my neck. The heat and pressure of the massage made my legs quiver.

God, that felt amazing.

Just like that, all my self-doubt slipped away like sand between fingers at the beach on a perfect day.

"That's better." He kissed my upper lip, then put both arms onto the floor to either side of me. I felt the weight of him on top of me and relished it. He kissed my closed eyes, then found my mouth again. "Much better."

"Are you ready for this, mystery dance partner?" Garrett flexed his cock. His massive length pushed steadily down my bare thigh, only a thin layer of fleece between us.

"Yes," I whispered. How long had it been? Six months? A year? I'd only had a few random hook ups since Doug and I ended things so long ago. Another burst of self-consciousness leaked out of me. "Why me? I'm no model or cheerleader."

Garrett regarded me curiously for a moment as he hovered over.

I immediately wished I hadn't said anything. Why couldn't I just enjoy myself? Was I so intent on sabotaging my happiness that I couldn't just keep my mouth shut and have amazing sex with a god like Garrett Walker?

"There are so many of them." He looked at me with honest, sincere eyes of the deepest blue I'd ever seen. "But only one of you."

I arched up and kissed him, not wanting him to see

the tears that were welling up in my eyes. I would enjoy this. *Every second of it.*

I reached down the ridges of his chest, my fingers dragging across hard muscle. Past the waistband of his thermals I felt the stem of his cock, then followed it further. Every inch I traced made my legs coil. I was so fucking wet. All I wanted was to feel him deep inside me.

He was so much bigger than in my dream. Even my imagination couldn't compare to the real thing.

He peeled back my towel. The winter chill nipped at me before being warmed by our bodies and the fire. He licked down my neck, then drew little rings around my nipples before catching them with his teeth and sucking them.

His cock throbbed at my touch. I couldn't fucking handle it anymore. I plunged my hand into his long johns and unleashed the massive beast. It slapped against my thigh and eager pussy, like it was spring loaded.

I bit my lip as I rolled my hand down his cock, the tip slick with precum. I gasped when he locked eyes with me again. I could see that he wanted me, and only me, in that moment. It felt incredible.

His fingers found my center. I was already soaked, but the way he stroked my clit made me even wetter. He rubbed the spongy head of his cock against my slit. Excitement bloomed in me like a brilliant flower.

I mouthed an unintelligible word when he slowly pushed the head inside me. The waves of pleasure that came with being widened made my eyes roll back in my head.

"You feel amazing," Garrett grunted, tilting his chin to the ceiling. I found a primal ecstasy on his face, when I found the strength to reopen my eyes. "I've wanted you for so long."

"Me too." I finally exhaled. Breathing took effort when he filled me up. I expanded around him like I was made for him. I loudly moaned when he finally hit the end of me.

He pivoted his hips and ground against me, somehow stimulating *all* of me.

Garrett let out a carnal grunt. His intense blue eyes were deep pools that threatened to drown me. The strength of his motion arched my back and dried out my throat. Impossible-to-reach zones within me awoke after years of neglect, and threatened to fold me in half with passion I didn't know I had.

My legs were useless. Having so much of him inside me made it too difficult to think, let alone move. Garrett planted one hand on the floor and the other on my inner thigh, squeezing it tight.

He lifted my leg over his shoulder. The movement opened me up so much that, I was immediately on the cusp of orgasm.

He pulsed, up and down, the ebb and flow of waves crashing. The sensation tore through me. It was a tornado of pleasure that made my core vibrate.

"You're amazing." My words came out in a daze between pants and moans.

He leaned back, not slowing the cataclysmic thrusting of his cock; he gently touched the side of my face. It was a sweet gesture. Seeing him on top of me, lit by the crackling fire light, warmed my soul.

His hand slid down my thigh before his thumb pushed slow circles into my clit as he fucked me. A wicked smile cracked across his face as he worked me inside and out.

"Fuck!" I panted. The pressure spilling over like a cup overfilled. My stomach crunched forward with climax, lifting my shoulders off the floor a little. I screamed hard and came even harder. "Fuck! I'm coming! Fuck!"

I was being fucked by Garrett Walker.

No. I was having sex with the mysterious stranger I met at the masquerade.

All my muscles went deathly rigid. Garrett pushed into me violently, as far as his hips would allow. His cock flexed in defiance of my crushing walls. I milked him as if my whole body were aching for his seed.

Garrett dripped with sweat. The fire made the droplets burst with color as they fell. He bared his lower teeth and dipped his head as his thrusting slowed. His thick cock throbbed, pulsated, and then finally exploded thick jets deep inside me.

He went to pull out, but I grabbed him, digging my nails into his waist. I needed to feel everything, every part of him. In my dream, we were more than just lovers. I wanted that, *craved it*, just for a moment.

The cold air made our sweat steam off our skin. Not even the fire could compare to the intense heat that blazed between us.

I slipped my arms around him and pulled him down on top of me. He enveloped me like a wet, sticky human blanket and littered me with hot, sensual kisses. Our limbs interwove. I didn't know where I began and he ended.

"Wow," I said, much later when I finally found my voice. "We must smell awful."

"It was good for me, too." He laughed, getting up to go clean himself off again. He walked about completely comfortable in his nudity, as if clothes were something of an afterthought. I wished I had his confidence.

"That's what I meant," I said.

It didn't hurt that he was amazingly easy on the eyes.

"It's no royal penthouse suite at the Hotel President Wilson in Switzerland, but..." Garrett smirked and made us a bed out of curtains and couch cushions. "I think we'll survive."

I tested the accommodations while he put enough wood on the fire to last us for most of the night. The bed wasn't so bad. Beneath the cushions was fairly new carpeting, so everything was soft enough to sleep on for one night. Garrett lay down, sliding a great arm beneath my back and curled me into him.

All his money, I smiled, *and he's sleeping on the floor with me.*

There was something incredibly romantic about that, even if I didn't know what exactly.

"What would've happened if we'd gotten that last dance together?" I asked, speaking of the masquerade party. The fatigue of the day, and the sex, had finally started to hit me once I was nestled against him. I wasn't going to last much longer.

"Everything," he said quietly. Exhaustion had finally snuck into his voice as well.

The sizzling and popping of the fire played just for us in our one perfect moment. He was right; I couldn't imagine anything ever being the same after this. I clung to wakefulness as long as I could, cherishing his arms around me and the enveloping feeling of complete protection.

I drifted to sleep not knowing what tomorrow would bring, but right now, I was safe, and I was loved.

For one night, we got to live that *other* life.

EIGHTEEN

GARRETT

With Judy naked in my arms, I watched the sun rise through the windows of the mountaintop lodge. The fiercely yellow light filled the room with a somber peace that I hadn't found in ages.

A peace I probably wouldn't have again for a long time.

The spent wood in the fireplace exhaled the last wispy gasps of last night and the warmth it shared. Judy stirred and turned her head away to shade her eyes from the creeping day. I pulled her into my chest to warm her against the nipping chill that invaded our little campsite.

Her blonde hair was plastered against my arm and her back was turned golden beneath an errant sunbeam. The beige linen curtain made her look like a Greek goddess come to earth in one of those old stories of forbidden love.

I'd never met a woman with so many shades of beauty.

I hadn't been able to sleep. There was far too much on my mind. I just lay there and carefully considered everything instead. Today I would have to give her and the whole town my decision.

Would I be their savior?

Jackie also fitfully ran circles in my head. I was worried about her. I was able to have someone let Michael know the situation. He was with Jackie and would let her know what happened. She probably cried when she heard the news.

The thought of Jackie in pain knotted my stomach.

Despite all that, I had a foreign sense of calm and... happiness.

The last time I'd spent the whole night with a woman was when I was still with my ex-wife, just after our daughter was born—back before everything soured between us. I'd been with hundreds of women in the years since and only now, with Judy, did I feel content.

I closed my eyes, feeling her weight and the rhythm of her breathing. I could just stay in this moment for the rest of my life and want for nothing. I fought to hang on to this instant, rip it out of time, and carry it with me like an old photograph.

The beating helicopter blades whirred with hummingbird speed and I knew the world had finally caught up with us. Judy groaned something about the noise.

"We're being rescued," I whispered softly, unable to keep the morning gruffness from my voice. "You might want to find some clothes."

Her eyes shot open several times before they were able to stay that way. "Now?"

"I certainly wouldn't mind another taste of last night." My lips grazed her forehead as I spoke. She wiggled slightly as the gravel in my voice coursed through her. "But this time, we'd have an audience."

"Shit. Okay." Judy sat up just as a medic tapped on the window by the front locked door. She gasped and jerked the curtain up to cover her bare chest. "Gah! Just a minute!"

I laughed, watching her pale skin grow hot with embarrassment. Now that he knew we were all right—better than *all right*—the medic cracked a smile, put up his hands in a gesture of apology, and backed away to give us our privacy.

"I just flashed a total stranger." Judy collapsed back into my arms, trying to hide. She was noticeably warmer.

"Scratch that one off the bucket list," I said. She thumped my chest with her fist.

"It's a good thing we're only doing three days," she said. "Things have a way of getting really crazy while you're around. First you ditch me, then you get into a fight with a rock star billionaire heir, and now... this. If we continued like this, tomorrow I might wake up on the International Space Station."

"Is that a warning or a dare?" I asked. "I might be able to pull some strings if you're interested."

Judy paused, no doubt wondering if I was being serious or not. "I need a shower and a coffee before I can even talk to you."

Soon enough, we were dressed and given a lift down to the base of the mountain.

The main lodge was ruined by fire. Whatever happened here, it was severe. Seeing the extensive damage, I felt much less annoyed that they had requisitioned my helicopter. Now I just hoped that no one had died in the accident.

My limo driver had been informed and was waiting for me. Judy's father was there as well and greeted her with a big hug. I got an urgent pang to do the same with my daughter.

I shook Paul's hand. I could see in his eyes that he wanted to scold me for ignoring the blizzard warning in the first place, but that was just as much the fault of the lodge as it was mine. Instead, he looked at me sternly and thanked me for taking care of Judy.

I nodded and told him I'd have my investment answer later today. I still needed time to think it over. With their only other form of tourism down for at least this season, maybe even next season as well, I knew that Caldwell Hope hung on the precipice of disaster.

Judy shook my hand and thanked me again. I wanted to sweep her up and kiss her, but the time for that had passed. It was already starting to feel like a lifetime ago that we explored each other's bodies and gave in to passion.

The ride back to my hotel was long and tiring. The heaviness of the decision I had to make, the exhaustion of the trek through the snow and lack of sleep, had all finally coalesced into a fatigue I hadn't felt since my last championship game.

No, it was much worse than that.

Football tired was a complete body-draining experience. Reliving a piece of my past with Judy was hard in an entirely different way. I was getting attached to her and that was dangerous.

I still had a job to do and a personal goal to meet. Would either of us survive my answer?

Michael met me at the door when I got in. I could tell by the redness around his eyes that I wasn't the only one tired from lack of sleep.

"She's all right," he said in lieu of greeting, knowing what I'd want to hear first. "I finally got her to bed a few hours ago."

"Did she stay up the whole night?"

"Yes." Michael yawned. "She was... distressed that

you weren't here. I don't know that the new medication is working, sir. Would you like me to contact Doctor—"

"No," I said flatly. I hated the fact that she was on medication at all. They said it was safe, and that it was necessary, but I wasn't so sure. It *dulled* her, and I didn't like that.

I sat by Jackie's bed, watching her sleep and thinking for a while.

Making time for my daughter wasn't the same as *spending* time with her. I wasn't giving her enough attention. I've been so focused on my goal that it eclipsed so many other things in my life.

But that would be over soon.

I checked my accounts and contracts yesterday. Everything was on track. As long as I didn't make any foolish mistakes, I would go down in history as the first person to hit thirty billion by my thirtieth birthday.

Eventually realizing that Jackie wasn't going to wake up soon, I kissed her on the forehead, whispered, "I love you," and let her sleep. I wanted to be the first thing she saw, but I didn't want to disturb her rest either.

When I left my daughter's room, Michael handed me a small stack of paper. "These are from the police, sir. Requisition forms, chopper inventory, and a full incident report. They request you take a look and see if all the information is accurate."

I sat on the couch and flipped through the pages,

barely skimming the information. I was way too tired for this shit.

"Also Moses Thomas Elementary School called," Michael said. "They'll resume classes after the weekend. They want to know when they should expect Jackie."

Stability. Jackie needed stability, especially considering her anxiety. That's why I never introduced her to any of the women I was seeing. I didn't want her to get attached. I fucked all that up with Judy.

They clicked really well together. The thought brought a smile to my heart, then a feeling of dread.

Jackie should never have met Judy in the first place. I was getting sloppy. I felt like I was coming apart at the seams.

"One train wreck at a time." I tossed the folder onto the table and rubbed my temples. "Give me the Cliffs-Notes on the ski resort. What the hell happened?"

"Negligence, sir," Michael said. He'd no doubt already proofread the entire thing and only offered it to me as a formality. "That's what it boils down to. Faulty craftsmanship, probably due to financial cut backs, followed by out-of-date inspections and a few well-placed lightning strikes. That's all it took for a five-alarm fire. Several were injured but, fortunately, there weren't any fatalities. And your helicopter wasn't damaged in any way."

What a disaster.

Something occurred to me that I was surprised I didn't know. "Which company owns the ski resort?"

"Not a company, sir. I keep finding the same signatures signing off on things. They're the same people who are overseeing the stadium construction."

"Fuck." I exhaled, rubbing my hands over my face. *Caldwell Hope owns it and the town council runs it.*

No wonder the damn thing caught fire. The local government was a joke. They green lit these massive projects, like the stadium, without the foresight and expertise to actually pull them off.

I worried that if I gave them money it would just be spent poorly, and I would never get a return on investment. That meant sacrificing my own goals. Could I really take that chance two months before my birthday?

"Get me a list of all the council members. I need to see who's making all these terrible decisions."

Michael disappeared into another room and returned a minute later with a manila folder. He handed it to me with a smirk. "I'd already taken the liberty, sir. Would you like a cup of coffee? Decaf?"

Of all of my assistants, Michael was by far the best. He thought the way I did.

I scanned the sheet of paper. Most of the names I didn't know. The dossier I'd read before was specifically on the stadium and its management. I groaned when I saw the name at the top of the list.

Paul Sullivan, chairman.

Judy's dad was the one behind everything. He was the final say as to what happened and what didn't in this town. That look earlier wasn't because he was angry at me; it was because he knew he'd screwed up.

"I'm going to need something a hell of a lot stronger than decaf." I stood up. It wasn't like I was going to get sleep any time soon. I grabbed an energy drink out of the fridge, popped the tab and took a sip. "Get me everything you can find on Paul Sullivan."

NINETEEN

JUDY

The sun dipped below the mountain where Garrett and I spent the night. My car slid on the snow as I hastily pulled into the mostly empty City Hall parking lot. Garrett's SUV limo was idling in the fire lane.

Garrett was giving his decision inside and I was running late! Monica was never going to let me hear the end of this. Punctuality was never my strong suit, but of all the times not to set an alarm....

Get your shit together, girl!

When I got home this morning, I was positively vibrating. I was glowing and floating. The thought of catching more sleep was impossible. I still felt his embrace, his hands holding me down and lifting me up. I was so inspired that I started another painting. It was an abstract piece with bold reds and thick, hard brush strokes. Above that were white sunbursts and blue speckles.

From memory I painted what I saw when I closed my eyes and he made me come.

And now because I was so involved with capturing my orgasm on canvas, I was late.

I grabbed my satchel and rushed inside.

The lobby was empty, which made sense because the building was technically closed. My low heels clicked quickly across the stone floor. It was a weird feeling seeing the abandoned counters and locked rooms as I made my way to my dad's office. I'd never been here on a Sunday before.

Dad had an office here because he had a hand in the public works development. He said it was closer to everyone, but I think he just preferred to work out of City Hall. It was where he would meet William King and discuss the future of Caldwell Hope.

Now that the ski resort was closed, what would happen if we never finished the stadium? Would City Hall look like this all the time? Empty and chilly—a monument of a better time when William King was still alive?

A chill of dread ran up my spine at the thought of Caldwell Hope going bankrupt.

No. Everything would work out. I took a deep breath

after stepping out of the elevator. Garrett would help us. I knew he would.

I glanced down to check my phone as I rounded the corner and collided with a wall. Or I would have, had the wall's big, strong arms not clamped down on my shoulders.

"Garrett." I smiled in surprise.

"Hi." His blue eyes snared me, but his melancholy smile made the hairs on the back of my neck rise. He wore a winter suit with a long, open jacket and a scarf that hung in two long lines from either side of his neck. He was dressed to combat the cold.

Was he leaving?

"I know I'm late, but I can't be *that* late. I got stuck behind a plow, then a school bus, and I swear I caught every light from—" I stopped myself from rambling, brushed a strand of hair back that slipped out from my wool hat in the haste, and re-centered myself. "That's not important. What happened?"

"Judy, I—" Garrett's handsome face hardened. The dimples in his cheeks disappeared, replaced by the muscles in his jaw clenching.

"You're not done already are you?" I asked. Worry was plastered across my face and I couldn't do anything to hide it. "What did you say? Did you say no?"

"I said yes."

Oh thank God. I exhaled relieved. "That's great!

Thank you so much. This is going to help so many peop—"

"Judy...." Garrett's lips became a tense line across his face. That wasn't a happy look. That wasn't the fairy-tale, everything-is-wonderful look that I was hoping for. "There were some non-negotiable stipulations."

"Like what?"

"I think it's best you go talk with your father. It's up to them now whether they want to accept my deal or not."

"Garrett...." My throat began to dry out. "Tell me."

Garrett paused. He regarded me carefully, like I was made of tissue paper and he didn't want to tear a hole in me.

"Your father," he said at last. "He must step down from stadium management for me to get involved."

"What? You want to fire my dad?" I staggered away from Garrett a step. "That's insane!"

"It's the only way."

"Do you have any idea what he's done for the people here?" I felt my spine heating up. A flush began to over-take me, and this time it had nothing to do with embarrassment. I was getting angry. "I don't care what the news said; it wasn't just William King who built this town. Dad worked just as hard. If anything, they were partners!"

"And without William King to temper and veto his

bad ideas, your father has had free reign to do whatever he wants. He's a self-made man and that's admirable, but he has no idea how to manage people or projects."

"Did you ever have any intention of actually helping, or was this all a game to you?"

"Judy, it's not like that."

"Not like what? What kind of monster are you, playing with all of us like that?"

"I'm willing to help." Garrett said, his cool eyes set, unwavering. "But I'm not willing to throw money away on a bad investment."

"My father is not a bad investment!" I pushed a finger into his massive chest. *How dare he.* "He's held that *elected* position for twenty years because he helps people. They want him. You're basically calling everyone in town an idiot."

"What if they are?" His voice was cold and dispassionate. The Grim Reaper had resurfaced. "Caldwell Hope was on the verge of collapse before I got here. Why do you think that is?"

"You think you know better?" I asked, heated. "I've lived here my whole life. You've been here for four days! In that time, all you've done is screw around and not take any of this seriously."

"I've done my research," Garrett said flatly and calm. "Have you?"

"You got what you came here for." I cut as deep as I

could, my anger blinding me. "Congratulations. You got to fuck the one girl that got away."

Garrett opened his mouth to reply but closed it again. A maelstrom of emotions flashed across his face, but I couldn't read any of them. Finally he closed his eyes and breathed heavily.

"It's better this way," he said, opening them again. The edge was gone from his tone; all that emotion drained from his voice. He looked me over one last time, then walked past me like I wasn't even there.

Garrett's hard-soled shoes echoed somberly down the hallway to the stairs. Only when he blinked out of sight did my anger start to subside. Once I heard my dad's name, I just lost it. I couldn't remember the last time I was so angry.

"He's out of his mind if he thinks I'm just going to give up my town." Dad was red-faced when I walked into his office. He was in the middle of a rant to no one in particular, just blind venting. "Billionaires have always thought the world was their play thing. I'm sick of it!"

Monica was silent, sitting cross-legged on the chair, taking in the spectacle.

"I know someone else that might be willing to help, now that Garrett Walker's offer is officially off the table," Monica said during a momentary reprieve from Dad's rant.

"Who would be crazy enough to invest this late in the game?" he balked, unbelieving.

Monica looked at him thoughtfully, then raised an eyebrow and curled her lips up on one side. It was a spiteful smile; there was no humor in it. It reminded me of a cat getting ready to pounce on a bird. It gave me a sinking feeling.

What if Garrett Walker was the *lesser* of two evils?

TWENTY

GARRETT

THE COOL BREEZE ROLLED OFF THE OCEAN, RUSTLING my linen shirt and shorts. A few weeks ago I'd been standing on a mountain with Judy where it was eight degrees outside. Now, I was on a different kind of mountain a few hours west in my jet, and it was almost eighty.

California weather, at least you never change.

The party in the mansion behind me spilled into one of the big pools. Most people here were high-profile celebrities, so it was easy to slip away without having a shitload of people falling all over me.

Jackie had resumed school, but she wasn't all that happy about it. She asked me about Judy almost every day. I never had a good answer for her. I knew this would happen. I never should have let them meet. I was careless, and now I'd brought more instability into my daughter's life.

I thought about Judy every day.

I needed to work harder at pushing her out of my mind. I was missing appointments and letting little things slip by me. I'd even lost a deal I had lined up. I didn't win them all, but this merger should've been a cake walk. It was starting to affect my work.

It was never going to work. How could it? I was brought in to pass judgment. I did what they wanted me to do. I passed a hand over my face to help me clear away the thoughts.

It's hard always being the bad guy.

"Reaper, my man!" Nate Goodman thumped a big hand on my back. At almost two-fifty shredded, I wasn't a small guy, but Nate made me look like a little kid. He had a hundred pounds on me and was Oakland's newest linebacker. "Shit... didn't expect you to make it."

"I couldn't play in the snow forever." I cracked a grin I didn't feel and shook his hand. Nate scoffed and pulled me in for a hug. It'd been a few weeks since I left Caldwell Hope, but I still felt like I needed a few dozen drinks to clear Judy from my mind. It never worked for long. "Congratulations on the contract, brother. That's more than my last one."

"The one you broke to run off and conquer the world?" He bellowed a great, chesty laugh.

It was a good thing I invested my money, because breaking a contract the way I did came with some serious repercussions. I had to pay a shitload in fines, and I would never be allowed to play on any NFL team again.

"Ain't no thing, baby." Nate straightened the pinstripe button-down shirt and fedora he wore. "I'm just a better ball player than you."

"Yeah?" I asked, dripping with pride. "How many MVPs do you have again?"

"I'm catching up, big man." Nate jogged in place to illustrate the point. "You better watch out."

"It'll be a cold day in hell when I can't outrun a linebacker."

"Yeah, yeah, yeah, fastest white boy in the league." Nate waved a dismissive hand.

"Bullshit," I corrected him. "Fastest *player* in the league."

"Maybe once." Nate laughed. "But Aaron Miller's got this new kid who just broke your record. You've been out of the game a long time now."

I'd heard about that. The son of a bitch gave him my jersey number. I didn't need Aaron Miller to make me feel shitty these days; lately I had more than enough practice. I glanced around Nate's property and changed the subject. "Nice place by the way."

"You have any trouble finding it?" Nate smiled wide. He knew I didn't have any trouble. The place was fucking enormous.

"You have two thirty-foot statues of weird dudes in

robes on either side of your driveway," I said incredulously. "No one has trouble finding this place."

"Argonath." Nate nodded, obviously pleased with himself.

"Argo-what now?" I exhaled, a little exasperated.

"The gates of Argonath." Nate's bright eyes lit up as his smile widened. "Isildur and Anárion: The Pillars of Kings." He gestured to the enormous statues. It was an odd sight, seeing a man that big become that animated.

I shrugged, having no idea what he was talking about.

"*Lord of the Rings*, baby!"

"Ah," I said, vaguely remembering that part from the movies. You'd never guess it to look at the man, but Nate was a huge nerd. "You're not still playing Dungeons and Dragons, are you?"

"Please." Nate looked insulted. "Twelfth level paladin, fifth level rogue dip." He brushed imaginary dust from his shoulders, then resumed his beaming grin. "The new game room is off the chain, man. I'm about to give some honeys a tour. You should tag along."

"Maybe later." I leaned on his balcony railing, watching the reflection of the moon ripple in the ocean. My body was here, but my head was in a mountaintop lodge with Judy Sullivan.

Nate cracked a beer and handed it to me, then opened one for himself. I took a sip and swallowed. It was bitter and tasted awful. I checked the label. Narragansett Beer. *What the hell was that?*

"You just signed a one-hundred-million-dollar contract. Why do you still drink this shit?"

"To remind me of where I come from." He turned to me, his perpetual smile shrinking to a knowing smirk. "They don't have 'Gannsett out here. I have to get it flown in from back home. Now, you gonna tell me what's on your mind?"

"Twelfth level paladins can't read minds?" I scoffed, taking another sip of the watery lager.

"Our spells aren't nearly that good," Nate replied, crestfallen, before narrowing his eyes at me. "Stop changing the subject. I can tell something happened."

"You remember the girl I told you about way back? The one I danced with at the Halloween ball?"

"The blonde with the nice legs?"

"Yeah," I said. I chugged the rest of the beer, then told Nate all about my trip to Caldwell Hope.

"Damn, man," Nate said, after about a half-hour recap and two more beers. "You still should've beat that King boy's ass."

"Nah, our kids were there."

"So she flipped her shit, huh?" Nate asked. "What'd you think was going to happen when you gave her an ultimatum like that?"

"What could I do?" I spread my hands then dropped

them. "Paul's got some good ideas, but he's in the wrong position. It's like if you tried to be a running back." I patted Nate's massive stomach.

He was the first to admit he was built for power not speed.

"How long are you going to torture yourself? What's it been, three years since Heidi died?"

"Four years and four months."

"That's what I'm talking about. You went on to do some good shit. No doubt. But you have to put the past behind you."

"I have," I said.

"You're so full of shit." Nate shook his head, seeing right through me. "Just because your dick gets a workout don't mean your heart gets one. Do you care about this Judy girl?"

"I don't know." I was good at so many things, but figuring out my feelings wasn't one of them. I thought about her all the time, especially after how things ended between us. But what did that really mean?

Nate whistled behind us, then waved some people over. I didn't bother to turn around until they arrived. It was a group of five women, a few of them were models and two I recognized were cheerleaders. All of them were in bikinis.

"This is my boy, Garrett." Nate introduced me to the girls. He rubbed his hands together and looked over each girl. They were all physically perfect in a Los Angeles sort of way. Big tits, toned everything, and a little too tan. "He's had a rough week. Who wants to cheer him up?"

They were all smiles as two girls draped themselves on my shoulders and the third, a short redhead, dragged a finger down my chest.

"Now you gotta ask yourself, G-dawg. What do you want more? This?" He nodded to the harem of girls hanging off me, then he threw his arms over the shoulders of the other two girls. "Or the snow bunny in that mountain town?"

The girls giggled and cooed around me, promising me things I'd had a thousand times before. I'd probably never even know their names.

Then I thought about the perfect moment in the morning right before we were rescued, when I had Judy in my arms. I could still feel her weight in my arms and smell her shampoo.

I caught the redhead's hand before it reached my belt. Nate raised an eyebrow at me, a slow smirk creasing his lips.

"Sorry, ladies," I said, breaking away from the girls, two of whom started to pout.

"I was hoping you'd say that." Nate nodded sagely.

"Oh yeah?" I asked. Nate was a bruiser through and through, but he also had a big heart. I was lucky to have him as a friend.

"More for me." Nate laughed heartily and took the other three girls in his massive arms. He was also an unrepentant whore. He took on a more serious tone. "Hey, either way, you gotta get your head straight. I heard about that last bank merger that fell through. The cutthroat Garrett Walker I know would've never let that shit slide. Get your head in the game or get your head out of it. This halfway shit isn't good for anybody. You've never been afraid of a fight, so stop being a little bitch."

"Why are we friends again?"

"Because I'm the only one who'll put up with your ass." Nate scoffed, then eyed me. "What are you still doing here? Don't you got a plane to catch?"

I chuckled to myself, feeling a little silly for not seeing the obvious answer. I couldn't run away from her. Not again. "Your beer still sucks."

"Haters," Nate said softly to his girls in a wounded voice. Then he nodded to me, winked, and led the women back inside. "C'mon, ladies, I'ma show you my game room. You can play with my minis."

TWENTY-ONE
JUDY

No. *Fucking*. Way.

I sat in the stall at work staring at a home pregnancy test, dumbfounded by the appearance of the second line. My hands were shaking. I was staring at the impossible.

My doctor's voice echoed relentlessly in my head. *"The fact that you survived was a miracle. I'm sorry, Ms. Sullivan. You'll never have children."*

Except this time, it was the carnival fun house backwards version....

How could I be possibly pregnant?

The ladies from accounting, marketing and sales, came and went in various packs. They touched up their makeup, used the toilets, and generally bitched about the latest rounds of layoffs and demotions to part-time status.

I was reminded that the rest of the world didn't start and stop when my life changed radically. It was just like last time. The pregnancy broke my already rocky relationship with Doug, but the miscarriage broke my heart.

And the rest of the world hardly noticed.

All this, and Garrett was gone.

I couldn't spend the rest of my life in the stadium office's bathroom. I didn't know what to do, or where to go, but I knew I couldn't stay in this damn place. I wrapped up the strip in a wad of toilet paper, then waited till the bathroom was empty before exiting the stall to throw it away.

I hadn't felt sick at all since we had sex. The only reason I even took this stupid test was because I was tired all the time and wanted to rule pregnancy out before I went to my doctor. I never had morning sickness, but seeing myself in the mirror made me feel nauseous.

Panic welled up within me. I couldn't go through another miscarriage. I refused to ever feel that way again. My mind was too scattered to even start to consider my options. An overwhelming sense of sadness and loneliness crushed me like a horse sitting on my chest.

I swallowed the lump in my throat, and splashed water on my face, not caring about my makeup.

What the fuck was I going to do?

I beelined from the bathroom to my new office. The sidelong glances I got along the way weren't because of my smudged mascara. They all hated me. *Even more now.*

Despite our new investor, Aaron Miller's grand speech about shoring up the holes in our community, and this stadium rising from the ashes, we were laying off people by the dozens. Hard working men and women lost their jobs, and I was given a corner office, a new title, a raise, *and* a secretary.

I went from being the boss's daughter to the boss. It was no wonder they hated me.

The sooner I could get out of here, the better.

The floor I was on was a ghost town. Only half the offices were filled, and a quarter of the employees who remained had been dropped to part-time or forced into becoming independent contractors. Aaron had done anything he could think of to screw people out of insurance and benefits.

Aaron Miller might be saving the stadium, but he wasn't saving the people who lived here.

When I approached, my secretary straightened and greeted me. She made a show of being extra cheerful now that the most recent round of layoffs probably got rid of a few of her friends. Victoria's brilliant, pearly smile was wide but nervous. It was obvious she was worried about her job. She was pretty, a little younger than me, and had a four-year-old daughter.

I'd come to realize that none of the pretty girls like Victoria had gotten fired. I could tell Aaron did that on purpose by the way he looked at them whenever he walked by. I didn't know if it was worse to tell Victoria that her job was secure as long as she looked good, or to keep the revelation to myself.

Either way I felt guilty.

But not guilty enough to quit, which was what I wanted to do.

I shoveled my laptop and a few other things into my bag, then grabbed my coat.

"Cuttin' out early, Jude?" came a familiar husky voice from just outside my open door.

I jerked to a stop.

Of all the investors Monica could get, I never in a million years thought we'd end up with Garrett's old football coach. I think the only reason Aaron was interested in this stadium was because Garrett turned it down.

I'd always made it a point to avoid Aaron Miller whenever possible. I'd only spoken to him once, and that was with my father right before I got the raise. If there was anyone I didn't want to see while on the verge of crying, it was him.

"I'm not feeling well, Mr. Miller." I smiled as politely as I could, despite the hair on my arms and neck standing on end.

Aaron was a short, fat man in his sixties who always wore a ball cap to hide his baldness. He wasn't technically the boss. The contract ensured that my father stayed on as general manager. That was just a title; everyone knew that Aaron had the real power.

"Hey now, Jude," Aaron said, putting a hand up and patting the air. "That's my papi's name. Call me Coach."

Jude. I hated that nickname and, because of it, I grew to hate the Beatles song it came from.

"Mr. Miller, I don't—"

"Uh." He cut me off with a raised hand. We waited in silence until I submitted to his *request.*

"Coach," I said, after taking a deep, resigned breath. "I don't feel well; I'm going to head home for the rest of the day."

"You do look emotional. That time of the month, huh?" He nodded as if immediately knowing the truth, regardless of what I would try to claim. He leaned on my desk and started carelessly rifling through the papers I hadn't filed yet.

"I know there's been a lot of changes this past week," he said, while casually glancing at my chest. "A lot of new policies goin' into effect. It's a lot for the fairer sex to process, especially during the time of month, when you're all...." He lewdly gestured toward my crotch. "Well, you know."

I zipped my coat up to my neck, suddenly feeling the need to be as covered as possible. Was this guy for real? I couldn't handle this right now. I just wanted to run out of the room screaming.

How had my life come to this?

"Point is. You take all the time you need, sugar."

"Why did you come in here?" I snapped at him. I'd had enough of his condescending tone. I remembered that without Aaron the whole stadium would close. Only then was I able to bite my tongue. "I mean... is there something I can help you with?"

Aaron frowned. "I was told that you were the *lucky* girl who showed Garrett Walker around." He let the words hang in the air as he walked about my office absently nudging and touching things.

Aaron definitely had obsessive compulsive disorder. He compulsively had to fix things. I could see how Garrett thought this man was a control freak. Since day one, Aaron made it perfectly clear that there was only one way to do things: his way.

"Did he like this town?" Aaron made a flippant circle with his hand. It was easy to see that he had no attachment to Caldwell Hope whatsoever.

"I guess," I said, pulling my bag closer to me. Hopefully he'd take the hint that I wanted to leave, but I doubted it. Or rather, I doubted he cared what I wanted.

"You two were busy. You went to that coffee shop, the amusement park, the King residence too, if I'm not mistaken. Then there was the ski resort." Aaron listed the places that Garrett and I went to. "I read about that one in the paper. So exciting!"

We weren't secretive about our meetings, but hearing him rattle them off so easily made my skin crawl. I shuddered to think of him actually spying on me.

"That's one way to describe it," I said, warily taking a few steps away from him.

Aaron wasn't a big man. I wasn't afraid that he'd over power me, or rape me or anything like that, but he completely creeped me out. With his pudgy cheeks, bushy unkempt eyebrows and angular nose, he reminded me of a small cruel bear.

By now we'd completely shifted places. He was behind my desk, where I normally was, and I was on the other side where people who visited me usually sat down. He swept a hand across the wood finish of my desk, then sat down in my chair with a grunt.

"When you were in that ski lodge all alone with him..." Finally he looked up at me and asked plainly, "... did you let him fuck you?"

My eyes narrowed. My pursed lips and knuckles went white from angry tension. The presumption infuriated me, but mostly I just felt sick. I forced back tears. I'd never let a man like this see me cry. I couldn't stop a renewed wave of nausea from rolling up my stomach and into my throat.

I burst from my office and stormed off down the hall. Victoria called out after me to see if I was all right. I couldn't speak. I had to ignore her. I didn't like the idea of leaving her alone with Aaron, but what could I do?

I couldn't even take care of myself.

The bathrooms were too far. The side effect of a series of layoffs was that there were plenty of empty offices. I thrust open the door to one then threw up into the wastebasket. I knew someone was bound to hear me, which was embarrassing enough, but at least I got the door closed in time.

I hated Garrett for what he'd done, but that couldn't dull the pain of missing him so much it hurt.

Where are you, Garrett?

Slumped down on my knees, broken, scared and in pain, I finally broke down in tears.

TWENTY-TWO

GARRETT

"WHAT THE FUCK IS THIS?" I STEPPED OUT OF THE limo and walked toward the Caldwell Hope stadium, except it wasn't called that any more. I was so surprised by what I saw that the limo had barely stopped when I got out of it. I nearly dropped the bouquet of white lilacs I'd brought for Judy.

Whoever the new investor was, he worked fast.

A lot of work had been done to it in the weeks I'd been gone. Like most stadiums, this was all massive sweeping glass curves and jutting angles. The surrounding grounds were packed to the gills with the infrastructure for restaurants, shops, a theater, and live bands to play. All of which was built with advertising space in mind.

Building an attraction hub that could be used, even while there weren't any games being played, was smart. I didn't have an issue with any of that. It was the other thing that chilled me even more than the cutting winter wind.

Reaper Stadium. The massive letters hung ominously above the gigantic Jumbo Tron screen. Below the letters was a pair of crossed scythes identical to the ones I had tattooed down my forearms.

Then things got even weirder.

It was the middle of the day, and work crews were crawling all over the place. I made my way down where the ticket checkers and security would be, then under the footbridge that connected the stands. I entered the stadium like every football fan would when it was complete.

Both sides of the main path were lined with ten-foot-tall standing Plexiglas-encased photographs of *me.*

They were stills of the great plays I made throughout the years. The first two were of me at a university in New Zealand catching the ball, back when I was tight end, before becoming a running back. The next two were of me in Minnesota, running the ball into the end zone. And so on they went. It was a highlight series of my entire career, up until my last game.

Was this some kind of sick joke?

They understood that I'd turned Paul's offer down, right? Was I in the Twilight Zone?

"Excuse me, sir." A construction foreman jogged up

to me. "This is an active work zone; you can't be here right now."

"I'm just headed to the offices to meet someone," I replied absently, still gaping at the images of me that were plastered everywhere. This whole place had my name and face all over it.

It was like a shrine to my honor.

When you played football, the contract you signed included likeness rights, so they could sell jerseys with your name on them and make video games with you in them. I'd have to ask my lawyers how legal this was.

This... was crazy.

"Oh shit!" the foreman said, wide-eyed. "I'm sorry. I didn't realize it was *you*. I'm a huge fan, man. Do you mind if I get a selfie with you? No one told me the owner was coming by today!"

Before I could answer, he already had his phone out and was taking a picture. I posed as patiently as I could, then made my way toward one of the staircases that would bring me to all the vending areas on the second level.

He thought I owned the place.

What kind of narcissist would build a monument to their own vanity like this? The whole thing made me furious.

The office entrances were under construction so I had to walk around the outer ring, past future restaurants and beer and merchandise vendors. The winter breeze mercilessly whipped through the long wide curved walkway. It was enough to make my eyes tear up.

I slowed to watch them lower the massive screen past the far end zone. To either side of the screen were walls of advertising, more than I'd ever seen at any other stadium. Aside from the near endless rows of block raised seats, you'd be hard pressed to find a square inch of the stadium that didn't have someone's logo on it.

My face and advertising, those two things were all over this stadium. I felt like I was a Nascar driver wearing one of those jumpsuits, covered head to toe in a patchwork of sponsors. The whole thing was such a chilling sensation.

I didn't like it at all.

"How do you like the memorial, Walker?" A voice split the howling wind.

I knew who it was before I turned around. How could I not? For better or worse, we'd spent years together. Most of that time was spent screaming at each other. Suddenly the ice in my veins melted and turned into molten lava.

With both gnarled hands planted firmly on the pommel of a cane, Aaron Miller didn't smile. He stared at me with the superiority of a rival who had the upper hand and knew it.

My boots clicked against the intricately laid stone walkway.

"Why?" I demanded, once I was close enough to be heard without yelling.

The old man came up to about the middle of my chest; I towered over him. Anyone else in his position would've pissed themselves at seeing an angry wall of muscle glaring down at them, but not Aaron Miller. His whole career had been spent gazing up to, and screaming at, giants even bigger than me.

"Nice flowers," he said, completely unconcerned. "They wouldn't happen to be for me, old friend?"

We'd never been friends. I knew my reputation. I was an elitist hothead who fought with everyone all the time. My teammates never minded my feuds and publicity stunts. It was all in good fun. It got the team fired up, and that got us to the championship.

Coach hated the antics, and me with them. To him, everything I did was an affront to the honor of the sport.

"Why?" I demanded again.

"Why *what* exactly?" Miller asked.

"Why the fuck are you here?" I demanded. "You run out of athletes to juice up?"

Miller's smug expression dissolved. That scandal finally got him kicked out of the league. He could never really fill the hole I left with another player, so he introduced steroids to a few of the guys.

After all his talk about honor, he was just as addicted to success as everyone else.

"I was hoping you'd stop by and see what I'd built." Miller waved his cane toward the grand entrance. "You passed up one hell of an opportunity here, Walker. Then again, you were always shortsighted. You never had an eye for the long game."

"Bullshit. This is a bad play and you know it. Saving this stadium, and this town, is going to cost way more than you're ever going to get back. Is all this just so you can recover your tarnished image? You going to be the one to swoop in and be the savior?"

"Savior?" He scoffed. His cheeks and double chin jiggled. "No. I'm going to squeeze this shit heap of a city for every penny it's worth, then sell it off piece by piece. Two years from now, it'll be another Detroit. Bankrupt and forgotten."

My eyes narrowed. "The public will crucify you for this."

"Me?" Miller placed a fat hand on his chest and feigned surprise. "Let me give you a lesson on Americans. Here, *seeing* is believing. Look around." He smiled like a bag of broken glass. "You see my picture anywhere?"

"There'll be a paper trail. Your fingerprints are all over this."

"You know who cares about that? Lawyers. I'm just a

silent investor, and everything I've done has been above board. There's nothing illegal happening here." Miller's cane menacingly tapped the ground as he walked a wide circle around me.

"As far as the public knows, you're the one who took a three-day vacation in serene Caldwell Hope," he continued, relishing the sound of his own voice. "You even saved poor Judy Sullivan on the mountain when the power went out. 'The ruthless Grim Reaper has a heart after all, and it belongs to Caldwell Hope.' That's what the article said, right?" Miller squinted against a gust of wind that blasted us, as if to punctuate his point.

"Memorial," I spat, remembering what he called the place earlier. It wasn't a stadium to him; it was a gravestone. "You're trying to bury me."

My leather gloves creaked from my fingers balling into fists. It wasn't just my hands either. My whole body tensed and flexed, like a coiled snake. My spine straightened, and my shoulders pulled back and down. I visibly grew wider and taller, further towering over the troll of a man.

My eyes flashed red. I felt the *old* me return. Back before they added "of Wall Street" to my nickname. Back when I was just the Grim Reaper. Back when I crushed people.

Miller smiled, poking a finger into my flexing form.

"And there's not a goddamned thing you can do to stop me."

I held his gaze, but said nothing.

What was I going to do? Hit him? I'd kill him. Then what? My life would be fucked, not to mention all the shit my daughter would have to go through. He knew I couldn't do anything to him. Even worse, he knew *I* knew that, too.

"You see, Garrett. I made you. I found you and plucked you out of the cesspit you grew up in. You were nothing without me." Miller's eyebrows furrowed, and for the first time, there was actual anger in his eyes. Old, deep-seated anger, like a scar that never healed right and constantly reopened. "And you broke your contract. No one ever breaks a contract with the league or with me."

"My wife died." The words dripped from my lips like venom.

"Boo-fuckin'-hoo." He dismissed my justification with a lewd wave of his hand. "Women come and go. I'm on my fifth marriage. Football was your *real* wife, and you abandoned her."

"There's more to life than this fucking game," I growled, barely containing my rage.

"No, there isn't!" Miller shouted, throwing his hands up. "You owe everything to this sport. It's what made you wealthy. Where would you be without it? You'd be just another one of these pissants!" He gestured to one of the construction guys pushing a full wheelbarrow far below us.

My parents weren't rich. I worked part-time as a construction laborer all through university to help them out. There was nothing wrong with getting your hands dirty from time to time. Sometimes it could even be the real measure of a man.

"I made you, billionaire." Aaron slammed a fist down into his open palm for emphasis. "I can unmake you."

"You won't get away with this." I forced the words through gritted teeth.

"There's nothing to get away with. I haven't done anything legally wrong. I'm giving these gullible fucks exactly what they want." He patted my shoulder. It was everything I could do not to take his fucking head off. Then as he walked away, he turned and said, "Send Judy my regards, will ya?"

THE GRAVELLY SOUND OF MY SHOE SLIDING AGAINST concrete alerted Garrett that he wasn't alone. Garrett turned defensively as if expecting that it was a fan among the workers looking for a selfie or an autograph with him. The expression on his face when he saw me melted his hesitance.

"Judy?" he asked carefully, as he walked around the large free-standing beer vendor kiosk toward me.

Did he actually recognize me or was he just hopeful? I was pretty bundled up. A tuft of my hair poked out the front of my fleece-lined hood, and my eyes were showing, but other than that I could've been anyone.

God, I felt horrible. I was just stopping to rest against the kiosk when I heard the talking. Then I didn't want to be caught eavesdropping, so I stayed quiet.

My stomach turned and I felt light-headed. Stopping

was a bad idea. I should've just run to my car. Now, I worried that I was too weak to drive.

It was freezing out. With the wind chill, it had to be ten below zero.

If it was so cold, then why was I sweating?

"Jesus, are you all right?" he asked when he reached me. He frowned, taking in the sight of me.

Did I look that bad?

The argument with Aaron Miller, his reputation, the fate of the town, all of that was brushed aside. There was only concern in his blue eyes. Concern and fear.

I was exhausted. Mascara streaked down my paler-than-normal face. It must've been easy to see that I was crying.

He touched my cheek, intent on rubbing the tears and black streaks away, but they were all dried. His eyes narrowed when he saw my pain as if they asked angrily, *who made her cry?*

I was still so angry at him for what he did, then for leaving altogether, but my head was swimming so much that I didn't care. I didn't trust him. I wasn't sure I even liked him, but part of me was always glad to see him. He exuded an aura of protection. I felt weirdly safer when he was around.

"Are those for me?" I asked, reaching for the beautiful long-stemmed white lilacs. I tried to remember the last time I'd received a gift like that. They smelled nice.

Had anyone ever given me flowers before?

Doug certainly never did. He barely even remembered my birthdays.

How fucking sad was that?

Garrett slipped a hand into my hood, then touched my forehead. "You're burning up. I'm taking you to a hospital."

Garrett swept me up with ease, cradling me and my bag. He took the stairs in twos and threes as he rushed me out to the parking lot. I felt like a little girl who'd fallen asleep in the car and was being carried to bed. I was out of it and scared about so many things, but being in his arms made me feel like I was going to be alright.

I loved that feeling. I teared up again. After these last few weeks, I needed this more than I could describe.

I was going to be all right.

"Garrett?" His name tumbled from my lips. I didn't know why I said it. It just felt good to say. It was reassuring. *I hate you, but I'm glad you're back.*

"Don't worry, dance partner." His softly accented voice warmed parts deep down inside of me I didn't know were cold. He kissed me gently on the forehead as he helped me into the car. "I'll take care of you."

I GASPED AWAKE, SWEATING AND DISORIENTED.

Where was I?

The room's lights were low, but as my eyes adjusted, I could quickly tell I was in a hospital bed. There weren't any clocks, but the windows in my room were dark. It must be late, or early. I couldn't tell which.

What happened to me?

Slowly the memories came back to me. I was at work and I felt awful, then that terrible man came into my office. Then... that's when it started to get fuzzy. I was outside.

What was I doing?

Garrett was there. That's right. I was listening to him argue with the new investor. I shivered, remembering now what they talked about. Aaron Miller never wanted to help us. That twisted asshole.

There was something else. Thinking straight was hard. My brain was oatmeal mush from whatever happened to me. It was like trying to remember the world through a kaleidoscope.

I threw up in an empty office, but before all of that....

I shot up in bed. Holy shit. *The pregnancy test!*

"You're awake," Garrett grumbled from a nearby chair. The deep baritone of his voice told me he'd been asleep for some time as well.

Had he stayed here with me?

"Did they say...?" I paused to collect my thoughts. "What did the doctors say?"

He stood up, stretched his hulking form and rubbed his eyes.

"You'd think with how cliché it is for someone to sleep in a bedside chair at a hospital, they'd at least make them more comfortable." He yawned, checked his watch, and then sat back down. "It was a fever. Doctor says you'll be fine."

My heart slid back down my throat. I sank into the bed. "What time is it?"

"Almost four."

"Please tell me you weren't here the whole time." I looked over at him.

Garrett looked *lived in*. He wasn't disheveled by any means, but he didn't have his usual crispness about him. His suit jacket was draped around the back of his chair, but his silk button-down was wrinkled and bunched in places. A pant leg was even rolled up to the mid-calf.

Who was I to talk?

I was in a hospital gown. My hair and makeup were a wreck, and I felt like a bag of garbage left out in the sun on a summer day.

"Of course not." He smoothed out the wrinkles in his suit and rubbed a hand through his hair. Then he looked up and smirked. "I tucked Jackie into bed a while back."

God, he even made unkempt look sexy.

"They just let you stay here? They only allow family to stay overnight here. What did you tell them? Because no one in their right mind would buy that we're siblings. How did you even—" I felt myself get spun up and slowed down. Talking was exhausting.

"They tried to stop me, but I can be pretty persuasive." Garrett's self-satisfied smirk fell away. "I called your father, but he wouldn't answer. Probably because he's still angry with me. I couldn't let you wake up alone. How are you feeling?"

"I've been better. Is there any water?" My throat was sandpaper and steel wool.

"The doctor insists on just ice until your nausea subsides." Garrett leaned forward in his chair and gave me a sympathetic look that crushed my soul. He was there, he saw and understood. His eyes told me that I would be all right.

"Thanks." I tried to force the grogginess from my head, but it was slow going. "For getting me to the hospital. I shouldn't have stopped where I did."

Garrett sighed; his lips became a thin line across his face. "How much of the argument between Aaron Miller and me did you hear?"

"Enough to know that he wants to destroy you and is willing to bankrupt us in the process."

"You should tell your father and the rest of the city council. The stadium isn't finished yet, they should still have the power to end Miller's contract. "

"He won't listen to me." I sank a little lower. I'd

always been a nuisance to him. Each job he'd given me has always been just to keep me out of trouble. "Dogs will fly the day he takes business advice from me. Besides, Aaron has gone out of his way to keep the mayor, and the rest of city council, satisfied.

"That evil sonofabitch knows exactly what he's doing." Garrett's eyes narrowed. Anyone could see that he really hated Aaron. "I don't know how yet, but I'm going to fix this, Judy. I promise."

"Stop it," I said finally. My heart was going to give out if he kept looking at me like that. Between the pregnancy test and everyone losing their jobs, I was too overwhelmed with everything to deal with all the emotions he stirred within me.

"Stop what?"

"Stop being so damn charming and compassionate. I can't handle it." I hated how hard it was to read him. To really *know* him. I'd seen so many different sides of Garrett over the course of knowing him that I didn't know what was real anymore. "You're a tornado, Garrett. You're this big, beautiful display of awe-inspiring power. You land in my life, turn everything upside down, and then leave." I started to shake my head but thought better of it. "And I'm left to just pick up the ruined remains."

"I'm sorry for how it ended last time." He frowned.

"An apology and some flowers? That's not good enough." I pushed myself up into a sitting position on my bed. The weakness and haziness in me started to dissipate. All the conflicting emotions swirled in my head and heart like a witch's brew. "You abandoned Caldwell Hope when it needed you most."

When I needed you most.

"And now," I continued, "we have something so much worse."

We sat in silence. Garrett appeared to run things over in his mind. I guess we both did, because neither of us talked for a few minutes. I wish I hadn't been so direct and harsh with him, but it was how I felt. I couldn't stop it from coming out the way it did.

"You're right." Garrett stood up and grabbed his coat. "I've gotten really good at running away from my problems. Words aren't going to make this right. I don't expect you to believe me when I tell you that this time I'm serious; that I came back for you and that I'm never going to leave you again."

"Garrett, wait. I—" I blurted, then abruptly caught myself. I desperately wanted to believe him, but how could I?

I hadn't even heard from him in weeks.

He paused and looked at me, patiently waiting to hear what I was going to say next.

Should I tell him I could be pregnant with his child? What if the test was a false positive? What if... I couldn't physically keep the baby? It was hideous to think about, but it happened before and it destroyed my relationship with Doug.

The thought of getting an abortion crushed me. I loved kids and always wanted one or two of my own. But what if my body just couldn't have children?

Everything frightened me, but the thought of giving up the slightest chance at a family terrified me. I shivered. There was no way; I had to at least try.

I'd never felt more lost and alone.

Looking into Garrett's piercing blue eyes didn't help at all. I didn't know what I had with Garrett, but for as angry as I was at him, I was terrified at the thought of him being out of my life forever. I chickened out and instead asked, "Where are you going?"

"I'm going to let actions show you the kind of man I am." Garrett charged out of the room like a white knight off to fight a dragon.

Oh, Garrett.... The cavalry rode over the hill too late this time. There was nothing he could do.

I pressed the button to summon the nurse. A few minutes later, a thin, tired-looking male nurse arrived with a clipboard and asked me how I was feeling.

"I think I'm all right. Or, at least, I'm getting there." I managed a weak smile at the nurse. It was all I could do to keep from crying. "Can you send the doctor in when she's free? I... I think I might be pregnant and I want to discuss options."

"Hi, Daddy," Jackie said, walking over to the couch I was sitting in front of. She held a bowl of cereal in both hands.

Despite all the pajamas I've bought her over the years, when it came to bedtime Jackie only ever wore an old band shirt that belonged to her mother. I remember making fun of Heidi for buying the vintage Aerosmith shirt, but now I'm glad she did. Jackie would never look cuter than she did right now.

But I wished she wouldn't cling to it. She didn't need an old shirt from someone she barely remembered; she needed to feel safe. I would move the earth itself for Jackie, but I couldn't be her mother too.

All the fancy doctors told me she needed stability. I'd come to realize that that wasn't enough. She needed something more....

"Why are you on the floor?" she asked, cradling her bowl of cereal as she got comfortable on the couch. The brown-hued milk from her Cocoa Puffs splashed every-where, leaving little stains that would have to be washed out later.

"It helps me think, coconut." I took the bowl and placed it on the coffee table next to me. "Eat over the table, please."

I was sitting cross-legged on the carpeting, typing away on my laptop. I hadn't slept, showered, or even changed clothes since I left the hospital. I was three coffees deep into GO mode. The dawn came and went, and I hadn't even noticed.

I had more important things to do.

They had given me the same hotel suite, which was fine. It was nice enough, and had the space I required. There wouldn't be time to work out this time around.

I needed to focus all of my energy on beating Aaron Miller.

Jackie turned the TV on and started watching cartoons as Michael walked into the room. He had a tablet under one arm and phone in the other hand. He'd been in the office researching legal loopholes, political back doors, and paperwork filing mistakes all morning.

"Anything?" I asked, rubbing my computer-fatigued eyes with dwindling hope.

"No, unfortunately. He's surprisingly squeaky clean," Michael said. He hesitated for a moment, then continued carefully. "I hate to remind you, sir, but if you go down this path and pursue a way to take over financial control of the stadium, you won't be able to hit your goal by your birthday, which will mean no world record."

That gave me pause. It was something I'd worked so hard for. With no more championships to win, that one goal was what pressed me onward.

Thirty under thirty.

"Should I keep digging, sir?" he asked.

I thought on it, unable to wrap my head around what I was giving up and for whom. This might be one of the biggest decisions of my life. I needed the opinion of someone I trusted, someone who knew me and Judy well, and was candid enough to speak their mind no matter how brutal the news.

"Coconut?" I asked my daughter, who was getting cereal everywhere but in her mouth. "Do you remember Daddy's friend Judy?"

Jackie nodded, smiling wide and showing off the gap where her big girl teeth had yet to arrive. "She knows magic. And she beat you in video games."

"She—" My lips pulled to one corner as my expression fell. "Daddy *let* Judy win a few games, so she wouldn't feel bad."

"She must feel great!" Jackie laughed.

"You traitor." I reached over and tickled her ribs. Jackie giggled and protested, but I easily scooped her up and sat her on my lap. I grabbed her bowl of cereal and put it on the coffee table next to us so she could still eat.

"Help me out, coconut. I need an expert opinion." I cleaned a dribble of milk off her chin. Having her this close to me reminded me how much she looked like Heidi. We probably never would've worked out, but I thank God every day that she brought Jackie into this world. "What's more important? Goals or friends?"

"Friends." She shoveled another spoonful of cereal into her mouth.

"Yeah? Why's that?"

"Because if you don't have friends, then who're you going to share your goals with?"

I let that one sink in.

I took a deep breath and looked up at Michael. My decision must have been written all over my face, because he just nodded and got to work.

"I should hire you to be a fortune cookie writer."

"I like cookies!" she triumphantly shouted, while simultaneously being distracted by the *Teenage Mutant Ninja Turtles* cartoon on TV.

"I know you do," I said, kissing her on the forehead.

Friends, I thought. Immediately it came to me. I

suddenly knew how I was going to beat Coach Aaron Miller. I was going to hit in the one place he protected most.

His pride.

And to do that, I was going to need a few friends.

A SHOWER, AND A FEW HOURS OF SLEEP, WAS ALL I needed to be put back in a good mood. I waited for the elevator at the stadium with a smile in my eyes. It wasn't a smile from a summer's day happiness but one born of rediscovered purpose. For the first time in months, I had a real, attainable goal. I felt like myself again.

I finally saw the battlefield, and had a plan of attack. I wasn't about to be caught off guard, not anymore. I was done playing defense.

There was a ding and the elevator door opened.

A few people in the middle of conversation shuffled out. Paul Sullivan alone remained.

"Garrett." Paul's voice was harsh and brief. It was almost as if he skipped right to the end of the conversation. "Going up?"

"Hi, Paul." I greeted him with a friendly air and walked in. "Offices please."

He nodded, pressing the button.

"Have you seen Judy yet?" I asked. "I heard she's been discharged."

I'd asked Michael to keep me informed as to her well-being. He told me that she was feeling better and was released. She just needed rest.

"Grabbing my things and heading over now."

We rode the rest of the way in silence.

"Paul," I said, stopping him from leaving when the door to his floor opened.

He begrudgingly turned around, then raised an eyebrow expectantly.

"It was... rude of me to be so short with you earlier. I apologize for the way I gave you my decision, especially the first time. That ball was a nice gesture."

Some of the disdain he had for me dissolved.

"From what Judy's told me," I continued, "you'd have made a great referee, you know that?"

"You think so?" His round face brightened.

I clasped the man on the shoulder and smiled. "Absolutely."

We nodded respectfully to one another as the elevator doors closed between us. Paul was a good man; he was just in the wrong position. Caldwell Hope had changed since William King's death. Paul needed to change with it.

When the doors reopened, it was a short walk to Aaron Miller's modest office. His secretary got up to ask me if I had an appointment, but I just winked at her and walked right in.

"What the hell do you want?" the short man began to roar. He didn't like surprises. "Brenda! Get me security!"

"Give me five minutes. You'll want to hear this, *Coach*." I punctuated the last word, like it left a bad taste in my mouth. In many ways it did.

Miller frowned, narrowing his eyes.

"Security will be here in three."

"Plenty of time." I sat down at the chair opposite his desk with a satisfied sigh, and crossed my leg. I had all the time in the world. "I have a proposition for you, more of a wager really. It's something that will put our rivalry to bed."

Miller looked skeptical. I could see the wheels turning in his head. For as much as I hated the man, I had to acknowledge his tactical prowess. He was an expert at planning, and was a master of the long game. But he was never very good at improvisation and spontaneity.

That's where I excelled.

That dynamic was what brought our team to the championships, over and over again. It's also the reason we'd always been adversaries instead of friends. I wasn't sure a man like him even had any friends.

Finally he sat down in his chair. He studied me for another moment, no doubt wondering what my angle was, then pulled a cigar from his desk and rolled it between his thumb and forefinger. "Go on then."

"I'm better than you," I said, interlacing my fingers together on my lap. My tone was even. I kept all emotion out of it. It was like I was telling someone what the weather was. "I always have been. If it wasn't you who recruited me, it would've been someone else. Without you I'd still have all my matching rings."

"This doesn't sound like a proposition." Miller's face began to redden, just like I knew it would. I'd almost forgotten how easy it was to rile him up. "You can get the fuck out of my office now. Hell, the next time you step foot in this stadium, I'll have you arrested for trespassing."

He glanced behind me and I knew that security had arrived to escort me out.

"My proposition," I said, raising my voice to capture his attention, "is proof."

Two armed men rushed into Miller's office. They were out of breath from running but tried not to show it. With one hand each on their holstered weapons, they asked me politely, yet forcefully, to come with them.

Miller held up a hand, stopping the men. "How do you mean proof?"

"The field is finished." I nodded over Aaron's shoulder. Behind him were windows that overlooked the inside of the stadium. "One game. Your coaching versus my team leadership. Winner takes all."

"All.... You mean the stadium?" he asked, a broad shark-like grin spread across his angular face. "And if I win? What could you possibly give to me?"

"You want to destroy my image? Well, I can do you one better. If you beat me, in a fair game, I'll petition to remove my nomination from the football Hall of Fame. You'll get to destroy my *legacy*."

Any player could opt out of the Hall of Fame if they wanted to. It's just that no one ever did. Why the hell would they? It was the highest honor an athlete could get. Giving this up would basically write me out of the history books.

I was right the first time I came to this town, when I told myself that my sacrifices were just beginning. I never would've thought I'd be making them for that silly masked girl I danced with so long ago.

Aaron Miller chopped the end off his cigar, lit it, puffing, and leaned back in his chair. He eyed me, carefully considering my proposal. Slow and deliberate. That's how he approached things.

"One week from today," he said finally. "I'm home. You're away."

"We'll see about that," I said, rising. "One last thing. I want Paul Sullivan to be the ref."

Miller's eyes narrowed. "Done. I'll have the contract drawn up and sent to you."

The security guards still escorted me out on Miller's orders. That was fine. I didn't mind the company. I'd gotten what I wanted. Now I just had to find players crazy enough to play for me.

I sighed. That might be easier said than done.

Paint spattered my hair and face, but I didn't care. Colored streaks ran up my hands and forearms as I put down long, aggressive brush strokes on the canvas in the far corner of my kitchen.

I'd been painting for days. My Spotify playlist blasted dubstep loud enough to drown out my cell phone. I was sad and angry, but above all I was tired.

Tired of feeling... tired.

In the days since the hospital, thoughts of Garrett Walker had infected my every waking moment. Sleep was the worst though. Every night I relived our night together in the lodge. Our naked writhing bodies searching one another, *completing* each other.

Then to wake up and not have *that,* emptied me out. My heart, and body, was an empty glass yearning to be filled.

So I turned my phone and my life off, and retreated to my apartment to do the only thing that ever made me feel better: painting.

I fell into my work. Once I got into the zone, there was nothing else in life except me, the canvas and the constant shifting sands of color. There was just something so visceral... so *primal.* All I needed was a paintbrush, and loud music to turn all the stress of my life off.

I mixed a light cobalt with French ultramarine blue, and tried it against the black pupils and whites of the rest of the eyes.

Damnit!

I sighed, cleaned off my pallet and reached for my mug of tea. I'd been trying for hours to get this color. *Why was it so fucking hard to find the right shade?*

It was only when I got the porcelain to my lips that I realized it was cold. When I breathed in, the pungent odor of mineral spirits punched me hard enough to make my eyes water.

"That wasn't tea at all!" My voice was drowned out by a vicious beat drop from my sound system. I chuckled to myself and shook my head as I reached for my *actual tea* cup. One of these days, I was going to be so tired, I'd really make that mistake. That would be a fun conversation with the nurse.

Empty. Damn.

Oh well. I yawned, stretched, and turned to walk

toward the kitchen to refill it from the hopefully still-fresh pot.

What time was it? I didn't realize how dark my house was until that very moment. I started painting in the late morning and only turned enough lights on to let me paint. My stomach must've passed out. When I stopped painting, it woke up with a vengeance and started growling. Takeout again? The thought didn't sound appealing. At this point I might be more fried rice than woman—

Oh my God! My heart leapt from my chest like I was a sinking ship.

"Ah!" I crashed right into the monstrous chest of an intruder!

I closed my eyes in shock and half jumped, half fell backwards, but his strong hands caught me. I thrashed in his iron grip. Spotify must have been watching this all go down, because the next song played was faster and more chaotic than any I'd heard previously.

What was I going to do?

Then, just like that, he let me go.

I stumbled back a step, then opened my eyes.

Garrett stood there in his fine suit, now ruined with wet paint from my thrashing. I exhaled in relief so hard, I almost hit the floor. I slapped at the space bar on my laptop and the music eventually cut out. The silence hummed in my ears, after it being so loud for so long.

"What the shit, man!" I pressed a hand to my chest

to help get my breath back. My lungs were full of fire and war drums. Thank God I was too young to have a heart attack. At least I *hoped* I was too young.

Garrett looked past me to the painting I was working on. He studied the portrait of himself. It was a dark spattering of reds and oranges, and in front of it was his form from the bare chest up. The background was abstract, but the foreground was photorealistic, as much as I could recall from memory.

Looking at him now, everything seemed right but the eyes. I was beginning to think there wasn't a pure enough blue paint to ever catch their hue.

"Your phone's been off for days," he said finally, still gazing at the painting. "I was worried about you."

Feeling embarrassed, I instinctively went to cover the canvas up. Because my studio was in my kitchen, my easel had two perpendicular bars welded onto the top. It was ugly. Like the-capital-letter-A-had-a-baby-with-the-capital-letter-T kind of ugly. But it let me throw a sheet over it when I had company, and not have to worry about the paint getting smudged.

He caught my hand and wrenched the cloth away, freeing the painting once more.

Then those unpaintable blue eyes turned their full attention on me.

"It's not what you think. I can explain—" But before I could get any more words out, he'd stepped forward, wrapped his big arms around my back, and lifted me into him. I was pulled right up off the ground.

Something primal came over him. He kissed me, long and hard. He smelled of musk and cinnamon, and tasted hot and savory. I closed my eyes, I didn't feel tired in his arms.

Garrett tore off his jacket and fitted shirt. What followed between us was a wild flurry of undressing. It was like a dam suddenly bursting. With raw, uncontained, urgent energy, we ripped each other's clothes off. His several-thousand-dollar suit, my thrift store painting outfit, it all became so much useless fabric falling into heaps around us.

My core tightened when I saw his massive defined pecs and shoulders. The heavy contrast of light spilling out from my studio, and darkness in the rest of my apartment, made him look like he was chiseled rock. When he flexed, his tattooed torso and arms came alive with color and motion. It was like the ink itself was putting on a show just for me.

I thought about my recent dream of him and me fucking in the masquerade ball. That man, that version of Garrett, didn't have any tattoos. I gasped in a breath at his lingering hand on my back. I liked this version much, much better.

I couldn't tear my eyes off his amazingly colorful body. His hips were sharply defined, and led my gaze down his insanely carved-out V in his lower stomach that ran into his boxer briefs.

This wasn't even fair. Garrett was almost over-whelmingly handsome.

Our passionate kisses couldn't be contained to each other's mouths. His lips searched the side of my face, and his teeth clicked against the studs in my ears. I let my head loll back and allowed myself to just feel his power wash over me.

With a smooth slide and jerk, he gently pulled my sports bra over my head. I'd have been more embarrassed about the unflattering top, or the broad-bottomed *comfy* panties I was wearing, but it was clear that Garrett didn't give a damn. He hardly even noticed any of that was there.

I had my arms around him but it wasn't enough. I needed to touch him more somehow. I wanted him to be the oxygen I breathed, and the blood in my veins. Then I remembered I was pregnant and a sudden fear blossomed inside me, like a dozen blood-red roses.

What if he doesn't want me? What if this is it between us? What if he thinks I'm just trying to get money from him?

No. Not right now. I squeezed him as he kissed my collarbone. If this was it, I was going to enjoy it.

I slid my hands down the bulging muscles of his sides. He was so warm; the grooves of his muscles were so defined. Guys never really looked like Garrett did. He was perfect. He was a rock star, an actor, he was every zero-body-fat athlete; he was impossible but somehow real. It was like being embraced by Michelangelo's *David*.

I glanced down to the massive bulge that pushed out his boxer briefs like a tent, and realized that's where the similarities to the statue ended. If David saw the huge cock that Garrett had, the statue would've broken down into tears.

The last time we had sex, I was sore for half a week. It was the best kind of pain... like going to the gym after a long time. My pussy and thighs were wonderfully sore, with little reminders of him, whenever I moved the wrong way.

In a tangled mess, we stumbled backward a few steps until we hit my kitchen table. He immediately hoisted me up with an arm, kissing down between my breasts. His chin was prickly with a few days of stubble; it scratched against my skin, as if telling me that even his love was rough.

The coarse hair would scratch me, and his tongue and lips would soothe away the pain. The lower he went, the more my body shivered and the wetter I became. I wrapped a leg around him, pushing myself into him. Instantly, lightning shot up my core.

Garrett moaned, feeling my wetness against his leg

and picked me up even higher. I was no anorexic twig model. I had some curves on me, but he moved me around like I was filled with cotton and feathers.

In a quick backward arc, I brushed all the clutter off the table. Half-finished projects, empty food boxes, clothes, mail, it all went crashing over the side. I wasn't sure why I did it. It just felt right.

Garrett must have felt it, too, because without a word, he tore my panties off and set me on the table.

Here, really? a kinky part of me gleefully cried. Aside from that lodge, I'd never had sex anywhere outside of a bedroom. He flashed those brilliant eyes up at me as he dropped to a knee before me. He made me feel so special, like I was the altar he was worshipping at.

Little tremors started deep within my thighs, as if my body knew what was coming and was trying to prepare for it. Seeing wasn't believing, *feeling* was. And right now little rockets were going off inside me.

I'd been so absorbed by painting and trying to forget everything earlier, I didn't realize how cool my apartment was. I felt that crispness over my entire body when Garrett leaned back to look at me, my nakedness fully on display.

In a bout of self-consciousness, I tried to shuffle back from the edge of the table and from Garrett. It'd been a long time since anyone went down on me. It was a little intimidating. What if he didn't like the way I tasted?

Jesus! When was the last time I'd taken a shower? I did some mental gymnastics and realized that, yes, I had taken a shower today. *Thank God.*

If he had any reservations, Garrett didn't show it. His strong hands clamped down on my thighs, preventing me from budging; his fingers pushed white indents into my skin. I liked the pressure.

His boiling hot tongue licked me from bottom to top. Spasms went off in me like popcorn being made.

It wasn't just the way his tongue and lips dragged across me that tore me to shreds, it was his eye contact. Two blue orbs, deeper than any ocean, looked into my soul as he ate my pussy. How could my body not crumble around that?

With every twist and suck, Garrett was *ruining* me. I almost hated him for it. At that moment, I knew I would never be able to fuck anyone else.

To say that Garrett made me moan would be criminally inaccurate. Garrett was a maestro, and my body was his symphony. His fingers pushed deep inside me, while his tongue drew hard designs into my clit.

He had me quivering so hard, my fucking bones rattled.

"Holy fucking hell!" I didn't know if it was the angle, the intensity, or just crazy skill, but I came like an earthquake. My hips bucked up, but he kept me grounded. If he hadn't been holding me, I'd have crashed through my ceiling. "I'm coming!"

Garrett slowed the pulsing rhythm but didn't stop.

I knew I was in trouble when his eyes flashed, and the corner of his mouth pulled up in a smirk. *I'm not done with you*, it said.

And holy hell was he not!

My hips bucked, my pussy trembled. I had almost no control, and that made it even hotter. I couldn't even touch myself this good. None of my boyfriends ever came close. The pressure within me immediately started building again. Another orgasm this soon?

No way.

Fucking *way*.

My hands snapped down on the edges of the table. I had to hold on for dear life. My body was tense enough to use as a diving board. I rode his mouth like a surfer rode waves. He brought me higher than I'd ever been, then crashed me back down. Slowing, pausing, pushing, and thrumming. Then when the wave broke he let me relax, but only for a moment.

During the final orgasm, when I was crashing, he bit one of my lower lips. I screamed in ecstasy and collapsed, writhing on the table, "No more! No more. I'm dying. You're killing me with your magical tongue."

I groped for him, trying to pull him up to me. I had no idea if the table would hold both our weights, and at that moment, I couldn't possibly care. Garrett kissed his way up the center of me until he reached my lips.

"I— Please," I stammered. I wanted more, and after that performance, he deserved to have me groveling before him. I just couldn't yet. Aside from Garrett, the last time I had sex was well over a year ago. It was like trying to run a marathon while only barely being able to jog. "I just need a minute to catch my breath."

"Sure," he said, picking me up off the table and carrying me into my bedroom.

Miraculously, my room was spotless. I had cleaned it a few days ago. I was actually in the process of cleaning my entire house before the surprise trip to the hospital put a stop to that. I wasn't expecting Garrett to come over, or even hoping that this would happen, but a girl could fantasize.

We relaxed on the bed quietly for a little while. It reminded me of my favorite part of the lodge experience. The sex was amazing, but just laying with Garrett made me feel so safe, so protected.

"How was it?" I asked finally, looking up at him. The soft light that flooded in from the other room, framed him in warm tones, making him look somehow softer. My body still vibrated with aftershocks that I hoped he couldn't feel. Garrett really did a number on me. "Being an A-list celebrity? You were everywhere for a while there. I even saw that terrible rom-com movie you made a cameo in."

"You saw *All the Wrong Moves*?" He eyed me skeptically, then chuckled. "You and five other people. I think it got a 10 percent on Rotten Tomatoes. They were being generous."

"You crashed through the couple's bedroom wall while they were finally about to have sex. You—you—you came in like the Kool-Aid Man and—" I lost it and started laughing my head off. The rest of the movie was completely forgettable, but not that part. Garrett's scene was the funniest thing I'd ever seen.

"And said—" Garrett cleared his throat and got into the exaggerated version of himself, with the super heavy New Zealand accent. "'Thirty minutes or the pizza's free. Dominoes don't fuck around.' Or something like that. I probably didn't say fuck."

"Yes!" I cheered, laughing so hard I could barely breathe. "Oh my God. That's perfect."

I loved every second of this.

"But to answer your question," he said, "it was great until it wasn't. That life put a lot of pressure on Heidi. Jealous people said some awful things about her. Then there were the games themselves."

"What about them?" My laughter faded. I wiped the tears from my eyes. "I saw an interview once. Fans were screaming your name. You were like a rock star."

"At home maybe, but away?" Garrett blew out his breath and cracked a smile born of exasperation. "Away, I was the most hated man to ever exist. Especially during my MVP years, while we were winning championships left and right. *People hated me.* They used to throw shit at me all the time. I had to start sneaking into the stadiums."

"No...."

"Oh, yeah." Garrett nodded, smiling wistfully at a life that must feel so far away now. "Someone once threw a beer-soaked pair of pants at me. Slapped me right in the face." He stopped so that my sudden laughing fit wouldn't drown out the rest of his story. "No one brings an extra pair of pants to a game, in the off chance that they see a hated rival player. It was a January game, too. That meant someone had to walk their flabby, naked ass out of that stadium in the freezing cold."

He pulled me into him so that I sat right before him. His arms wrapped around my stomach and his chin rested on my shoulder. He was my big spoon. I could feel the baritone treble in his voice through my spine. It was like he crawled into me in a whole different way.

This, I thought, *I want this. This is* all *I want.* Closeness, caring, and concern were such small things, but they meant the world to me. Why couldn't I have this? I only wanted it for the rest of my life.

Is that so much to ask?

"Are you back?" I turned to face him, realizing that the moment had to end at some point, and I couldn't live with not knowing the truth. I traced the thin line of cadmium yellow paint that ran down his chest, smudging it into his coarse tuft of hair. "I mean really, *really* back? I can't go through losing you for a third time."

"I'm here." He glanced down at the yellow smear on his chest, then looked at me. Those hard blue eyes stared directly into my soul. "I'm yours and you're mine."

"Good." I twisted myself around to press the side of my face into his chest. I tried to bury myself and hide from his intense gaze. I took a deep breath and swallowed, then finally told him what's been on my mind for weeks. "Because I'm pregnant."

There was no gasp of surprise or questions. He didn't pull away to criticize or berate me for lying to him about not being able to have kids. He didn't even try to run away. In fact, he didn't do anything, which made me even more nervous.

Had he not heard me? Or worse, did he fall asleep? I really didn't want to have to say that out loud a second time. I could only pour out so much of my heart.

"Jackie's going to love having a little brother or sister," Garrett finally said.

The dam behind my eyes broke and I immediately started to cry. It wasn't tears of happiness, but tears of *relief.* I'd been holding my breath since the miscarriage so long ago, and now I could finally breathe again.

Garrett nudged my wet mess of a face up to look at him. God, I must've looked like such a wreck. He didn't care. His smile was soft, and extended all the way into those deep blue eyes. Those *light azure* eyes.

That's what color they were!

"You're mine, Judy." He drew a thumb down my cheek, wiping away the rivulets of tears that refused to stop. "Now and always."

I squeezed him as tight as I could and let myself believe. I couldn't answer him. I could barely even breathe. The loneliness I'd felt for so long was gone. Was this what Gloria and Molly felt with the King brothers? God, I hoped so.

Had I finally found my happy ending?

No, I realized. *This was my happy beginning.*

I'm going to be a father again. The thought crashed into me, over and over, as I held Judy tightly on that queen-sized bed.

I absolutely loved the thought of all this. It felt like I had a family again. That ignited something in me that I thought was gone forever. I would always love Jackie, and we were a family, but this was different.

Having both Jackie and Judy was such a *fuller* experience.

I decided then and there that I was going to marry Judy. I was going to make her mine, in every way possible. I was going to take her body and her heart, and in exchange, give her all my love and my last name.

We could do whatever we wanted together, go anywhere, and see everything. She would be by my side forever, and we'd watch our children grow and find love themselves.

Fuck. That was all so corny!

But goddamn if it didn't sound amazing in my head. It was what I wanted with Heidi, but that was all just a show for Jackie toward the end. We could barely stand each other anymore. Heidi wasn't the right one, but I was still glad for our time together. It gave me Jackie, and I wouldn't trade her for the world.

And now I was going to have another kid. The smile hadn't left my lips since Judy told me she was pregnant. "Do you want a boy or a girl?"

"Healthy. That's what I want." There was a tinge of sadness to her voice that crushed me.

"You said before that you couldn't have kids?"

"I couldn't. I mean, apparently I can get pregnant like a champ." She tried for a weak smile, but it was gone in a heartbeat. "I don't know. I—" She cut off to drag her hands over her face and exhale. This was obviously extremely difficult for her.

"Did something happen?" Something definitely happened. Rather, it was gently finding out *what* happened. I wasn't going to force her. She could tell me in her own time, in her own way.

"Miscarriage," Judy said with a heavy sigh. It was easy to see how heavily it weighed on her. "The doctor told me it was a miracle I was even able to get pregnant in the first place. They diagnosed me with polycystic ovaries. He encouraged adoption."

Judy went quiet for a little while. I didn't say anything either, but I pulled her in as tightly as I could. I wanted to remind her that she wasn't alone. I didn't need words for that.

"That was the last nail in the coffin with Doug I think." She started again. "Although, honestly? The relationship had soured long before that." Judy paused again for a time. There was no rush, no reason not to give her all the time in the world.

I'd have given her the rest of my life if that's what she needed.

"She'd... have been around the same age as Jackie, I think." Her voice choked off at the end.

I slid out from behind her and planted my elbow on the bed to properly look at her. Judy covered her eyes right away but still couldn't stem the tide of tears from driving down her cheeks.

"I don't care what the doctor says." I brushed her cheek with my thumb and pulled back one of her hands. I wanted her to see my concern; I wanted her to feel that I was here for her, and that I wouldn't let her go through this alone. "There's nothing wrong with you."

"What if I can't keep it? What if—" She gasped in air to keep herself from crying harder.

"It won't come to that, I promise."

"That's a promise even you can't keep," she said darkly.

"You're right. But what I can promise is that I'll be right there with you every step of the way. I'll send you to the best doctors in the world. Your pain is now my pain." I stared as deeply as I could into her sad green eyes. I wished I could pour the certainty I felt into her. I wanted to wash away all her old emotional scars. "I love you."

Her eyes widened. Neither of us saw that coming. Just because it was a surprise, didn't mean I meant it any less. I did love her. I think a part of me even loved her all the way back at that masquerade party.

She was that missing part of my soul that refused to be filled with anything but her. I felt like a fool for not realizing it until now. I'd achieved so much; I was wealthy in so many ways for so long, but so incredibly poor in love.

Not anymore.

I lowered my lips onto hers and kissed her. The salt from her tears made the whole thing feel real. Real love wasn't always roses and beauty. Sometimes it was pain and tears, and vulnerability. Sometimes it was wet crying kisses.

"I love you, too," she said in between kisses and sobs, her lips frantically searching mine. As she shifted for a better position, her arm slipped out and punched over a stack of art books and romance novels she kept on her bedside table. They clattered noisily across the floor. She wrapped her arms around me and started to laugh at her clumsiness. "I'm sorry I'm such a mess of a person."

"You are a beautiful disaster," I said, pulling back enough to clear the last of the tears from her face. "But I wouldn't have you any other way."

"How are you even real?" Judy smiled in disbelief and edged out from under me.

"I could ask you the same thing." I grabbed her and pulled her on top of me. Her blonde hair fell around me in sheets as she giggled and half-heartedly protested. "So many people in my professional life are so two-dimensional that they put cardboard cutouts to shame."

"Well, I'll have you know that I can knock things over in all three dimensions." Judy raised an eyebrow and nodded. She propped herself up, arching her back and flipped her hair over her smooth shoulder.

The light in the other room bathed her naked form with a warm glow. I studied her every curve from her collarbones down to her hips. Every delicious inch of her was stunning. The engine inside me, the one that had brought her to the brink of so many orgasms, switched back on and was starting to hum.

Soon it would rumble.

"What else can you do?" I asked, sliding a hand up from her stomach to between her breasts. My palm was big enough to devour all of her cleavage, and my fingers were long so that my thumb and pinky could reach both her perky pink nipples.

The weight she wore around her heart was lifted and was finally written on her face. Her tears were dry and wiped away, and she didn't have any makeup on so aside from her eyes being a little puffy, you wouldn't be able to tell that she'd been crying at all. That warmed my heart, because that meant I was doing something right.

I liked that feeling.

"I can return the favor." On her wrist, Judy wore a purple hair elastic; and with a few well-practiced movements, she had it all tucked behind her in a high and tight ponytail. Her full tits bounced as she swayed and swished the ponytail behind her.

Watching her made my lower stomach tighten with desire. Judy sat on my lap and grinded her ass against my thighs. Her hot, wet pussy blazed against my skin. It stoked a furnace in me that was still warm with embers, from when I went down on her. Under her pressure, my cotton boxers started to stretch and expand as my cock pushed down my leg.

I could still taste her on my tongue. It made me almost drunk for more. I wanted to split her legs to the side like a birthday present and fuck her so hard she wouldn't be able to sit down for a week without remembering my long, hard cock inside her.

I didn't realize how much my balls ached for her until she slipped off me completely. I involuntarily crunched up toward her when she pulled down the last piece of clothing between us. Like a metal beam under pressure, my cock sprang to life now it was freed from its cotton prison.

"Jesus." Her eyes flared when she saw it. My cock was long enough that it slapped against my belly button when it was released. "Good thing I wasn't too close! You'll take an eye out with that thing."

I moaned, flexing against her, growing harder and fatter as she grabbed my cock in her hands and squeezed. Even with two hands, she could barely contain me. Fuck I loved the sight of her cresting the tip, then plunging back down to the base.

There was only one thing better than that.

As if she'd read my mind, Judy crawled further down the bed enough so she could place the very tip of her tongue on the head of my swollen cock. I folded her pillow and shoved it behind my head. I wanted to watch every second of the show.

Teasingly, her plump lips smacked off the head of my cock.

"Now." I groaned. My balls pulsed in uncomfortable anticipation "That's not fair."

Judy smiled, kissing again. "Since when does the Grim Reaper of yadda yadda yadda care what's fair?"

"You make a valid point." I dragged my hand up the back of her head and pushed her down on my cock.

Judy's eyes flashed again, resisting for a second, then cracked a grin and dove in herself. She parted her hot lips and took as much of my cock into her mouth as she could without choking. Her hot tongue slid around my fat girth, licking and sucking.

I took one of her hands and started jerking myself off to show her how I liked it. Judy caught on immediately and put both hands to work, squeezing up and down my long shaft. She knew what she wanted and went for it. Judy was incredible; it was like her hands were made for my cock.

I wanted to let her bring me all the way, let her suck my soul out of my cock. It wasn't long before she made me want to blow. I wanted to blast my hot seed down her throat more than anything.

Almost anything.

I grabbed her ponytail like a handle and pulled. There was popping sound and a long line of saliva as she came off my cock.

"Did I do something wrong?" She looked up at me with a hint of self-consciousness.

"No," I said, easily flipping her onto her back. She bounced on the bed, her tits jiggling seductively. I moaned at the sight of her. My engine was white hot. I was primed and ready to let loose on her. "If anything, you were too good."

I put her on her back and threw one of her legs over each of my shoulders. My cock bobbed between her thighs. I grabbed the base of my length and slapped it against her hungry clit.

"Oh fuck." Judy's chin pushed up toward the ceiling, and her eyes rolled into the back of her head. Her slit parted greedily, ready for me. And fuck was she wet.

I bit into her leg as I pushed myself in. My head and shaft disappeared inside her. Her breathing was sharp and shallow. The walls of her pussy had to stretch to fit me, so I went slow enough to not hurt her.

When I bottomed out deep inside, I didn't pull out. Not just yet. I leaned forward to nearly lie on top of her. Her legs came with me, lifting her ass slightly up off the bed. I squeezed her tit in one hand and pinched her nipple in the other.

"Do you like that?"

Judy bit her lip and nodded eagerly.

I licked the nipple I'd been pinching, and she squeaked. The lick turned into a suck, as I slowly started to pull my cock out. Her nails dug into my back, slowing me even more. When I got most of the way out, I pushed back in a little faster. She crushed her walls all around me as I did, the pressure heavenly.

I developed a rhythm where I gradually picked up

speed with the thrusts. I felt every inch of her sliding over for me, yielding for me; it made my head swim. My lips, and occasionally teeth, switched from nipple to nipple to chest, then to neck as I fucked her.

I slid my hand down her curves, finally resting at the nook I made at her waist. I squeezed her side and ass tight, anchoring myself, and my cock, into a faster, harder rhythm.

Judy moaned my name. Not loud at first. She could barely draw in enough air to make out the words, but the closer she got to coming again, the easier and louder her voice returned to her.

"Fuckfuckfuckfuck! I can't even!" Judy's whole body vibrated and jerked with ecstasy. When I briefly let go of her waist and slapped her ass, she screamed in delight.

The bed rocked under the force of our fucking. It slammed into the wall over and over. It was lucky she didn't have any neighbors. I couldn't believe how good she felt. I wasn't just fucking the girl I danced with so long ago and couldn't stop thinking about.

I was fucking the mother of my child.

I was... making love.

"Oh oh oh fuck!" Judy's body went stone rigid, then shivered, from the back of her neck to her pointed toes, as the orgasm rippled through her. "I'm coming. Fuck me, I'm coming!"

I kissed her chin, tasting sweat, either hers or mine. It

didn't matter. We were one in so many ways. And now we even came together as well. Her bone-rattling orgasm was the final straw that pushed me over the edge.

I dropped my head to her chest that was spotted with paint and sweat. I pumped my seed deep into her; my balls quivered as they unloaded in blissful release. I came so hard I had to shut my eyes.

What was this woman doing to me?

"Fuck me." I collapsed on top of her, letting her legs slip off my shoulders. I pulled out and laid next to her, exhausted. My adrenaline drained away with my cum. I realized just how tired I was. I hadn't really slept in days. I was too worried about making things right with Judy.

I didn't care what any doctor said. If she wasn't pregnant before, she sure as fuck was now.

"What now?" Judy asked distantly. We both just went through so much, that it wasn't all that surprising she'd have a lot on her mind.

The bed was a wreck. The covers, sheets, and pillows were all on the floor. Even the fitted sheet had been come undone and was partly wrapped around my leg.

"Now?" I slid my arm under her and pulled her sweaty body against mine. Her pulse had just stopped racing, and her breathing was only finally slowing as well. I was a force to be reckoned with before, and that was before I felt as whole as I did now. "We kick that piece-of-shit Aaron Miller out and save your damn town."

Judy's lips pulled to one side. It was one of her tells, the expression only happened when she was uncertain. Something was wrong.

"Can we...," she asked with upturned eyes. "Can we take showers before we save the town? We're pretty fucking gross."

"Cole Briggs will be landing in fifteen minutes, sir," Michael said from the other side of the office in my hotel suite. We'd been at it all week; Judy started calling players with us, asking for their help.

Cutting it close, Cole.

We were building a team for one game only. And that game was tomorrow night.

It was like fantasy football, only with real players and a hell of a lot of real money being spent. All the best guys were still playing, vying to be one of the last two teams for the championship.

It was slow going. Most of my own teammates were scattered all over; a few had retired, and one had even died. For all the glitz and glamour, professional football was a dangerous career. So many concussions and brain damage. For my daughter's sake, I was glad I got out when I did.

"And Nate Goodman?"

Michael checked his watch. "About four more hours till he arrives. He'll be the last one. We have our team, sir. Well, mostly." Michael corrected himself.

We were still a man down, but that was the best we were going to get. I'd found out that Aaron Miller had been paying off, or threatening, players I'd contacted. He'd been undermining me at every turn.

"Good work, Michael." I got up and stretched, tired from staring into computer screens and countless phone calls. "Let Byron know I'm on my way down, then take the rest of the night off."

"Byron left feeling ill, sir. Another chauffeur will be ready and waiting."

I nodded to Michael and made my way to the living room. I personally went to pick up each player that flew in. It was the least I could do for them agreeing to come out and play on such short notice.

I stopped and hovered in the doorway behind the kitchen. I got a full view of Judy playing *Minecraft* with Jackie. The sight made my heart soar. Jackie was giving her a virtual tour of the house she built in the video game.

"This is your room." Jackie beamed, moving her avatar around the moss-covered stone bedroom. It was about an hour before her bedtime and, for the first time ever, Jackie wasn't wearing one of Heidi's old shirts. She wore these Batgirl onesie pajamas that Judy picked up for her. "I made a fireplace, and a water elevator, and a thing that makes cakes, then shoots them."

I didn't know if it meant real psychological growth for her in coping with the loss of her mother, but it sure felt like it. It was clear to see that Judy filled a void in her life that Jackie desperately needed. I couldn't believe I almost robbed her of that.

"I get my own room?" Judy asked excitedly. "Sweet!" She of course wore her pair of Batgirl pajamas, too, so they matched.

There were so many terrible things I wanted to do to her in those black-and-yellow pajamas. She anticipated that, or was hopeful of the foreplay, because she bought a second pair for when she actually went to bed.

"It's nighttime now. Wanna go out and fight monsters?"

"Oh, I was born to fight monsters." Judy glanced over and saw me smiling at her. "You've got some levels; you should enchant your armor and sword first. I'll be right back."

I loved watching her walk over to me, knowing that she was all mine. She made me feel so strong and awake when she was around. Judy was a kid at heart, which was great because I wasn't. We were like puzzle pieces from different boxes that inexplicably fit together perfectly.

These past few days with her were incredible. There was a lot of work to do getting a team together, but in the brief interludes in between, life with her came alive. It was never like this with Heidi, even during the good times. Judy and I clicked.

We'd taken a break last night to watch *The Grinch* as a family. It made sense with Christmas being a few days away. Jackie had fallen asleep on the floor at our feet. There was a part toward the end of that film where the narrator says, "the Grinch's heart grew three sizes." Well, that's how it felt every time I looked at Judy now. My heart was full enough to burst from my chest and explode into fireworks.

"Are you going out again?" Judy asked, draping herself across me.

"I am." I spoke the words with my lips just grazing hers. The quiver raced through her back and down her thighs. I wanted to trace it with my tongue.

Michael came out of the office and set up his laptop like he always did when I had to leave Jackie for a business meeting. A thought rocketed through me. It made me extremely nervous.

"Would you—" Did I really want to do this? The thought of having a woman I liked watch my daughter scared me. It was a completely irrational fear because I trusted Judy with my life. As a parent though, trusting anyone to care for your child is a nerve-wracking experience.

I took in Judy's emerald eyes, letting her soft, genuine gaze wrap around my very soul. The fear and uncertainty that filled me whenever I thought about my daughter's safety drained away. I didn't have to worry anymore about who to trust with Jackie. I now had Judy by my side. *Things are just the way I want them. Finally.*

"Would you mind watching Jackie?" I asked Judy.

"Not at all." Her eyes flashed in surprise. She knew how big of a deal this was for me to ask. Trust was difficult for me, and faith in someone was nearly impossible. "We're going to kill some monsters together." She shrugged, then smiled. "Maybe go find the Ender Dragon. No big deal."

Her breath was the strawberries they had for a snack. I licked the taste of the sweet berries from her lips, and enveloped her in a big hug. Her blonde hair cascaded over my shoulder, allowing me to drink in the scent of her conditioner. *Now,* I thought. *Now my life is perfect.*

"Gross!" Jackie called out in disgust. She tugged on Judy's blouse. "The monsters are waiting. Let's go."

"Be careful of those monsters," I said, kissing Judy before my excited daughter dragged her away.

I basked in the glow of that moment before I left. I'd always thought it would be father and daughter for the rest of my life, but now with Judy, I realized how much better a full family could be.

It wasn't nearly as bad during the drive as the blizzard that stranded Judy and me at the top of the mountain, but the snow was heavy enough to slow Cole's jet's arrival. I greeted the big linebacker right on the long air strip when he exited the jet. That was a luxury afforded us by using a private airport in the next town over. It's also where I kept my helicopter.

Fuck the TSA.

The first thing I'd done when I became wealthy was ensure I'd never have to walk through another airport security line ever again.

Cole, like my buddy Nate, was the size of a Volkswagen beetle put up on one end. He was amped up and half in the bag from a poker game in Vegas he'd just left. The linebackers were my favorite guys to hang out with when I was on the team. I didn't know if it was because of all the shots to the head each of them took, but they were always a riot.

He was telling me this story about our old quarterback, Willy, when my limo pulled away from the airport on its way back to our hotel.

Back to Judy.

It was impossible to not fall in love with that thought. Judy and Jackie were waiting for me. I couldn't think of a more perfect reason to go home. It was amazing to me that I could consider any hotel room—granted a really nice one—*home*. I knew it had nothing to do with the building; it was all about the people inside it.

Love. It was a multifaceted emotion. One I never thought I'd ever explore the depth of beyond Jackie. But here was Judy bringing me to an entirely different level.

"I shit you not, man," said the six-foot-tall, corn-fed Milwaukee giant, pulling me from my daydream. "After he finishes fucking the girl, Willy tells her he's gotta go. The dude then goes right to her husband's barber shop for his haircut appointment.

"While he's getting the fade done in the back—you remember the one he always got, right? Said his initials and shit. So the barber is finishing up when the chick's panties fall out of his pocket." Cole roared. He was laughing so hard he struggled to get the words out. His laughter and general mirth were more infectious than anyone else's I'd ever known. He was the kind of guy who always slapped your shoulder when he reached the end of a story. "He knew they were his wife's because her initials were embroidered on them!"

I smiled, shaking my head. I wish I could say I was surprised. Willy was a gifted QB, but he was dumber than a sack of hammers.

"The old man kicked the shit out of him, then and there." Cole wore a big dopey grin as another bout of hysterical laughter overtook him. He wiped at the tears in his eyes, "Still... still... he still had the fucking hair gown thing on!"

"The barber's apron?" I asked and Cole nodded, which made me chuckle even harder. "He was just lucky he didn't ask for a straight razor shave that day. Why the hell did he take the girl's panties?"

Cole started several times but couldn't get the words out. He was cracking himself up too much. "The motherfucker keeps a collection—"

Then the world turned inside out.

Tinted windows at night meant we couldn't see who just crashed into us. Everything happened so fast that I doubted we'd have been able to react even if we could see them. Like a film reel missing frames, my memory of what came next was as jumpy as a bad YouTube clip.

There was an impact about halfway down the limo. The vehicle lurched hard, the driver's side wheels popped up off the ground. The interior of the limo was suddenly a shotgun blast of shrapnel from all the broken glass and everything else that wasn't strapped down. Neither of us was belted in; Cole and I were thrown like stuffed animals.

I didn't know exactly what finally pushed us off the road: the crash, the snow, the road's sloped median, or maybe it was the combined five hundred pounds of grade-A, NFL beef flying through the inside of the cabin.

It didn't matter. The next thing I knew we were upside down, then the car started to roll sideways. I had no idea if we were careening down the side of a hill, a valley, or if we'd just been pushed off a fucking mountain. I blacked out long before we finally landed.

The last conscious thought I had wasn't about whether I would survive or not, or my goal to be the youngest person to hit thirty billion.

My daughter's face flashed in my mind, then Judy's sparkling emerald eyes. *In another life we'd have gotten one more dance.*

WHEN GARRETT PUSHED OPEN THE DOOR THAT morning, I was finally able to swallow my heart; it had been lodged in my throat all night. I wanted to meet him at the hospital when I found out what happened, but he asked me to stay with Jackie so she wouldn't wake up afraid.

Michael was in tow with a bag of whatever the doctor had given Garrett. Garrett nodded to him, and Michael immediately started calling people, then disappeared into the office. He probably went off to inform everyone about the car accident.

"You look terrible!" I rushed to him and hugged him as carefully as I could. Garrett's left arm was in a sling and he was covered in bruises. The crash broke his arm. There was no way he was going to be able to play the game tonight. "Are you all right? You're obviously not, but are you going to be okay? What did the doctors say?"

Michael forwarded a copy of the police report but, because we weren't married, I couldn't get anything out of the doctors. The police report read like a summer movie blockbuster. I actually gasped out loud several times while reading it.

On their way back from the airport, Garrett's limo was T-boned by another vehicle. The only one that could've gotten a good look at the assailant was the limo driver, but he was in a coma.

Somehow, with a broken arm, Garrett pried open the wrecked door and carried the driver up a one-hundred-yard embankment in hip-deep snow. Then went back for his friend Cole and did the same thing.

"The Armani isn't one of my favorites, but 'terrible' is a bit harsh." As far as changes of clothes from a hospital stay went, most people went with sweats or jeans or something else simple, but not Garrett. Garrett was dressed in a pinstripe suit, white French-cuffed button-down shirt, and a silver vest. No tie though.

"You know what I mean, you jerk." I punched him in the good arm, then immediately felt bad about it. He didn't seem to mind; he just hugged me tightly and kissed me.

A night's worth of pent-up worry and tension suddenly drained out of me. It felt like I'd spent hours standing on my tiptoes, and only now I could finally relax. It was one thing to hear that everything was fine, but another thing entirely to see it with your own eyes.

He was going to be okay.

"It looks worse than it is," Garrett said. He frowned bitterly and looked away. It was easy to see he was pissed off and upset. "Cole's down for the count though. His leg is broken in three places."

"It's not your fault, you know." I dipped my head to the side to look into his eyes. "I'm sure Cole knows that, too."

"Daddy!" a little voice cried out and charged us. We kept the serious details from her, but there was no hiding her concern when she saw her father in the cast and sling. "You're hurt."

"It's just a scratch, coconut. Don't worry. I'm tough." Garrett bent down and picked her up easily with his good arm. He kissed her on the forehead and smiled a big, goofy grin, which made her giggle.

I followed him into the large, open living room. The sun was just above the balcony windows which colored the room in a fiery rose hue. Jackie's toys from the morning were littered all over the place, like a minefield. Given what was happening with her father, I didn't have the heart to ask her to put anything away.

"Can I draw on your cast?" Jackie's face lit up.

"Of course you can. Go find your markers." He set

her back down and squeezed her shoulder, before she could run off excitedly.

He was so good with her. I loved seeing those two together.

There was a pounding on the door so loud, I expected it to crash open any second. Michael jogged over and answered it, before it was ripped from the hinges. A massive form pushed past Michael and stormed into the apartment.

Michael threw his hands up in a defeated shrug that made me chuckle. Without an elephant gun, there was literally no way Michael could've stopped this man from doing anything.

"Damn, man! What does it take to kill you?" the big man asked. He was a giant in every way. I'd seen a picture of Nate Goodman before, but I could never have imagined he'd be that big. He had to be part rhinoceros.

Were all linebackers this big?

"I'm not all that eager to find out." Garrett got up and did the thing where they slap shake each other's hand, and pull into a hug. Nate was careful not to hit Garrett's wounded arm. Garrett turned back to me and introduced us. "Nate, this is Judy."

"Hello, miss." Nate politely shook my hand, then turned to Garrett and gave him the impressed "not bad" frown. I beamed, despite myself. Garrett had been talking about me; that somehow made things between us feel even more official.

I decided to step away and get us all some drinks. I'd read the police report and was pretty caught up to date with everything that happened. Honestly, hearing it once was bad enough to make me a little squeamish.

I just got Garrett back, so the thought of losing him scared the hell out of me.

When I came back, they were still talking about the accident.

"That greasy-ass motherfucker," Nate growled with balled fists. "You're sure it's him?"

"I can't prove it." Garrett thanked me for the coffee and continued, "But yeah, I'm pretty sure it was Aaron."

"Woah, what?" I sat on the couch next to Garrett, searching his and Nate's faces for answers. "I thought it was just a car accident. Are you talking about attempted murder?"

"I can't find my markers," Jackie whined, storming into the room. "I can't find them!"

Talk about a complete one-eighty. I switched into what Molly called parent mode and buried my fear and anger under a happier façade, so as not to scare Jackie.

"We'll get you some more later," I said, pinching at her belly. She protested but smiled, not able to hold onto her anger. Seeing her on the verge of a giggle fit actually made me feel a little better. I was always impressed with

Jackie's timing. No one could diffuse a serious, intimate, or angry situation faster than her.

"Hey there, little Reaper! You remember me?" Nate asked with a big grin.

Jackie shook her head, obviously a little intimidated by seeing such a large man. That was certainly understandable. I could barely get over how big Nate was, let alone a seven-year-old.

"What? Aw, man...." Nate shot Garrett a disappointed glare, shaking his head. "Some friend you are."

Garrett shrugged.

"Do you want to see my *Minecraft* house?" Jackie asked innocently. Whatever fear she had about Nate's size didn't stand a chance next to a child's willingness to play. "I built all of it."

"Hell yeah, I do!" Nate sat cross-legged next to Jackie on the floor by the massive TV as she powered on the Xbox. The controller looked so tiny in his hands. "Hold up a sec. I gotta log in first. Can't be missing out on any of them achievements, know what I mean?"

The adorable display almost made me forget what we were talking about.

"Can we get back to the attempted murder part, please?" I asked Garrett in whispered tones, as the soothing *Minecraft* music came on. Hearing myself talk about something so criminal made my chest twist up.

The next town over could be a shitshow from time to

time, and occasionally some of it would spill over here, but even then it wasn't that bad. We had some trouble with tourists being dicks once in a while. Usually it was just drunken idiots doing drunken-idiot things, but it was mostly harmless. Nothing too hardcore ever really happened in Caldwell Hope.

Nothing like attempted murder!

"I can't prove it was him," Garrett repeated, placing his hand on my knee to reassure me. It didn't work.

"What if Aaron wants to... finish the job? What about me and Jackie? Are we in danger?" Worry crept up my spine. All my problems and concerns seemed so petty in the face of actual death.

"I doubt it. I don't even think he was trying to hurt me. Not really."

"You're joking?" I went all wide-eyed, and anger flared within me. I couldn't stand the idea of a weasel like Aaron doing something like this to the man I loved.

It was also frustrating that Garrett didn't seem to be taking this seriously. Was I just overreacting? I paused to consider that.

Fuck no!

Aaron was a monster for what he'd done to Garrett, and what he was trying to do to my town. It was unfair, and he had to be punished for it.

"Garrett, he smashed your car—" My voice doubled in volume. Garrett snapped a glance over at Jackie, but fortunately she was too absorbed in her game to hear us. I dropped my voice back into a whisper. I loved kids, but I still had so much to learn now that they were going to be a real part of my life. "Sorry. Sorry." I took a breath. "He put you into a ravine! He broke your arm. This is crazy. We have to call the cops and have him arrested."

"Neither Cole nor I actually saw anything. There's nothing we can do until the driver wakes up." Garrett leaned back on the couch and stared off into the middle distance. His eyes narrowed as he mulled something over. "There was no way Aaron could've known I'd be in that car. He's trying to weaken my team, put more stress on me and hope I crack." There was a long pause. "No," he continued. "He's not trying to hurt me. He's trying to beat me. And he can't do that if I'm too hurt to play."

"You're not going to play, right?" I didn't like where this conversation was headed. "Right? Garrett—"

"I don't have a choice." Garrett got up. His blue eyes darkened with deadly seriousness. "I made you a promise."

"You have a broken arm! We can find another way to kick Aaron out and save the town!" I felt frantic. I couldn't let him do this. There had to be another way. Even if he was right, this was insane.

"Yeah?" Garrett asked. "I'm all ears."

I opened my mouth to speak, but my throat went dry. I couldn't think of any alternatives. Aaron had made sure to keep all the town officials happy. There would be no reason for them to cancel their contract with him. He went to all the meetings, told his smiling lies about helping the town evolve and flourish, and started the funding that would finish the stadium.

What they didn't see was the way Aaron had already started cannibalizing us to sponsors. Soon Caldwell Hope would be one big gentrified strip mall with all our uniqueness torn away. Then the bankruptcies would start.

Still, there had to be another way. Garrett might not have shown it, but he was in an incredible amount of pain. He needed bed rest not touchdowns.

"Nate, help me out here," I pleaded to the big man on the floor. "He can't possibly play like this."

"He's only a running back. They don't need both arms." Nate winked at me, smirking, and handed the controller back to Jackie. "Now a linebacker... that's a real job. 'Specially being that we're down two guys."

I glared at Nate, who playfully recoiled, throwing his hands up in a don't-hurt-me gesture.

"Aaron is an excellent tactician. He's covered his tracks." Garrett guided my face back to his with a finger beneath my chin, then he kissed me. His two days of stubble scratched lightly against my lips. "It's his scheming against my skill and leadership. I'll be fine, Judy."

"I want to believe you. I really do." My voice tapered off in a breathy whisper that made my heart hurt. It was all I could do not to cry. Images of him getting seriously injured, or killed, out on the field picked away at my brain like desert vultures.

Garrett grabbed my hand and tightly squeezed, then he flashed me a warm, honest, reassuring smile. *Don't worry*, it said. *Trust me.*

I did trust him, of course, but that's what made me worry.

I watched him and Nate leave for the stadium. Six hours till kickoff; it was a criminally short amount of time to determine the fates of the man I loved and the town I called home.

Were we really doing this? The fate of thousands of people was resting on a single football game.

I sat there lost in thought, the endless tapping of Jackie mining cobblestone in the game was my only company. I felt helpless. Garrett didn't even live here and he was risking so much. And what was I doing?

If this insanity was actually going to happen, then I couldn't just stand aside and watch. I had to do something. A new resolve washed over me as I considered my options, eventually something clicked.

I snapped up my phone.

"Hello?"

"Gloria, I need your help. I have the biggest favor, to end all favors, to ask you."

"Okay...." Gloria's curious smile came through in the sound of her voice. Her newborn baby cried in the background as if she already knew why I called. "What's the favor?"

"You're not going to believe this," I started. "Are you sitting down?"

THIRTY

GARRETT

Paul blew the whistle, ending the play. He and my teammates rushed to get all the other players off me. I was at the bottom of a tackle pile in the other team's end zone. Last play before the half, and I was smashed into the fucking bedrock.

At least I'm warm. I would've laughed, but I was pretty sure one of my ribs was broken.

I'd snuck through a hole in their defensive line and snagged us a touchdown, but that wasn't going to be enough. We still trailed by fourteen points, and the hits just kept on coming. Every time I turned around, there was three hundred pounds of angry asshole looking to cave my skull in.

The only thing that kept me from passing out was the agonizing pain in my left arm. We held our own and made them fight for every yard, but at the cost of getting the shit kicked out of us. Being outnumbered was a lot harder than I thought.

I impressed myself at how fast and tricky I was after all these years, but the other team was just fucking everywhere, especially number fifty-three. All the skill in the world couldn't change the hard truth that this kid was just younger and faster than I was. The fact that he had my old number wasn't an accident.

What I wouldn't give to have Cole out here guarding my ass right now.

On his way up, number fifty-three put his knee into my side hard enough to knock the wind out of me. "Coach Miller sends his regards."

Nate shoved the kid off me with the might of a man who could easily flip cars onto their sides. If it were anyone else, they would've been eating dirt, but fifty-three jumped into a back roll and popped right up unfazed. Nate couldn't hide his surprise at the kid's agility.

We were in serious trouble.

"You all right?" Nate asked, helping me up. His voice was nearly drowned out by the crowd's lingering ooooohhhs at the last play's especially hard impact. A few more hits like that one, and it wouldn't matter how many Advil I popped like Skittles; soon I just wouldn't be able to get back up.

Only a quarter of the seats were finished enough for

the public to use, but they were packed, the occupants energetic enough to fill the whole stadium with noise. There was no advertising done for the event. That didn't stop word of mouth from bringing several thousand people together last minute to watch what was being called a practice game.

I was reminded just how much of a draw this stadium was going to be when it was finished. Caldwell Hope had a lot of potential, if it was handled correctly. This town really could be something great.

"This whole thing... went differently in my head... on the way over," I said, in between sucking in air.

"No shit." Nate grabbed my hand and pulled me to my feet. My head spun with the sudden motion. Now that I was standing up, I could see how exhausted he was. Nate was damn good at what he did, but he was only one guy. Aaron took advantage of his superior numbers and put two guys on him and two on me.

My teammates jumped up all around and hugged me. After the game we'd been playing, our morale seriously needed that touchdown.

"How's the arm?" Nate asked after the celebration had died down. He was still catching his breath from the last play.

"Still there, I think." That last tackle loosened the mount enough that I could wiggle my arm, which sent searing pain shooting into my shoulder. Despite countless objections, the doctor's armored it up as much as they could and pinned it to my chest.

"C'mon, boss man," Nate said, leading me off the field to the locker room with all the other guys. "You can sleep when you're dead, and it ain't past your bedtime yet."

Judy sat in the first row of seats by the southeast corner near the player's entrance tunnel. She was wearing a white puffer because of the bitter cold, and it reminded me of how overdressed she was when I took her to the coffee shop on that first date. The memory brought a smile to my face. This was the right thing to do. It was hard, and it was painful, but seeing her there cheering for me made me feel warm deep down. Seeing her took the chill out of my soul.

I waved at her on my way past. It took everything out of me to pretend I wasn't as hurt as I was, but it felt like someone threw me in a drying machine with a bunch of rocks and broken glass.

Inside the locker room, a battery of doctors and physical trainers looked us over and patched everyone back up as best they could. Aside from reaffixing the hard and soft bandages that pinned my arm to my chest, my doctor mostly shook his head and tried to dissuade me from continuing. "You can add three cracked ribs to your growing list of injuries, Garrett."

"That explains why it hurts to breathe." I gritted my

teeth and pushed through the pain. I made it clear that come hell or high water, I was going to finish the game.

"Don't you have a daughter?" Doc was trying to use psychological warfare on me. The unspoken question was really, "What would she think of the needless risk you're taking?" I didn't answer. Eventually he sighed and placed a bottle of Vicodin on the bench beside me.

Drugs: The second-best thing to good advice.

"If you keep playing like this, you won't need me. You'll need a mortician." Doc shook his head, grabbed his medical bag, and moved on to the next player.

I took the bottle, rolling it around in my hands, and stared down at the smiley face Jackie had drawn on my cast before we left. I was teaching Jackie every day, whether I liked it or not. What would today's lesson be?

If you're stubborn enough, you might just get yourself killed?

What was the alternative? To give up when things got hard?

I looked around. It wasn't just Nate and me. Everyone was pretty beat up. The players bitched and moaned about us getting our asses handed to us, looking generally miserable as they did it. In my entire career, I'd never seen morale lower than it was right now.

I shook my head. I refused to teach my daughter that the things you loved weren't worth fighting for. I'd much rather finish what I started and be in danger than not be able to look her in the eyes when I safely ran away.

This was something I had to do. All I could do is pray Jackie and Judy forgave me for it.

"Hey!" I shouted. With great difficulty, I climbed up on the bench to speak to my team.

"Listen up!" Nate boomed, backing me up.

"Someone once told me you can't take a championship with a bad team," I started, despite not having everyone's the full attention. "We haven't played together in a long-ass time, but I've bled with each and every one of you at one time or another. Just because we've had our balls kicked in, doesn't make us a bad team."

"Yo, Garrett, man." Marcos, our tight end spoke up. He wore a black eye from an elbow that knocked his helmet clean off earlier in the game. "I appreciate what you tryin' to do here, man, but this is some fuckin' bullshit! These guys are fuckin' animals. They ain't playin' the same game we playin', man."

There was a general murmur of agreement with him. Marcos was right. I didn't know where Aaron got these guys, but most of them had to be college athletes, because I didn't recognize many of them. They weren't as skilled as us, but they were fast, strong, and had endless endurance.

And Aaron trained them to be extra violent.

"Do any of you know what we're even doing here?" I asked.

"Yeah, we're gettin' our asses beat," someone chimed in.

"This is more than just playing a game or making a paycheck." I walked down the length of the bench. Fuck, I was sore. "This is more than even beating that piece-of-shit Aaron Miller. You see all those people out there in the freezing cold? This is for them!"

I hadn't won them over, but at least that quieted the room. They were at least listening to me, which meant they hadn't given up completely yet.

"This is about every fan that ever paid to see you play." I grabbed the jersey of the closest player. "This is for every little boy or girl who wears your numbers religiously. They watch you play, and it gives them hope for what they can achieve in their future. They look up to us, especially those that don't have much else.

"Most of you have worked under Aaron Miller in the past. You know he's ruthless, single-minded, and will do anything it takes to win. How many of you has he fucked over in that process?" I looked around, seeing more than a few heads lower. That last remark hit close to home for a lot of the guys here. "Championships come and go. I've got four rings, and I would trade them all in a heartbeat to know my daughter had a safe place to grow up.

"Caldwell Hope is a town of three hundred thousand people. Good people. They're on the brink of bankruptcy, and Aaron Miller running things is only going to make life worse for them. We all saw what happened to Detroit. Well, the same thing's going to happen here."

I let the implication breathe as I walked around the room. There were a few players here that grew up in Detroit and knew how hard of a city that was to grow up in.

"Tomorrow you all get to go home, but for these people, this town is all they have. They can't run away and hide in their mansions. We're just football players, but today... right now, we get to be more than that. We can be heroes!"

The mood had begun to shift. It was slow, but I could see energy returning to the room. Chests started to puff up and postures straightened as they slowly began to stand up. These were all good men who just needed to understand what they were really fighting for.

"This game doesn't mean a goddamned thing for us, but winning it today for them out there means everything! You want to give back to the people who made your dream possible? Really give back?" I looked around. Everyone was on their feet. All eyes were glued on me. I'd finally pushed past their wounded pride; I could see the fire of defiance in them.

It was savage and hungry and wasn't going to take shit from anyone.

We weren't football players in that moment. We were warriors.

"Well this is how we fucking do it!" I screamed, pounding my bandaged-up shoulder. The adrenaline that coursed through me was better than any drug. I was going to save Judy's town like I promised her. It didn't matter that we were outnumbered. For her, I'd play ten-to-one if I had to.

A wave of roars rang out in the locker room as the team went nuts. They punched walls and smashed into each other. The testosterone and killer instinct were so thick that it made the air steam. My guys were frenzied, angry, and ready to go out there and make Aaron Miller's team bleed.

Nate led the charge back onto the field. I picked up the rear, psyching up as many of my guys individually as I could. I had to double back for my Vicodin when we got out of the locker room. It didn't matter how amped up I was from the speech and excitement, there was no way in hell I was leaving that behind.

By the time I made it back out into the tunnel, I found Aaron Miller waiting for me. He wasn't stupid enough to let my team see him when they were practically frothing at the mouth; he must have entered from a maintenance door.

"Nice speech, son. Really..." Aaron waved his hands in a circular motion as if reeling the words out of his head on a silk thread. "...really rousing."

"Don't you have your own team to harass?" I crunched a Vicodin in my teeth to deal with a sharp surge of pain at seeing the man.

"You know I don't make speeches, son." Aaron lit up his cigar, drawing in air with puffs to get the cherry end bright and red. He smirked through great billowing exhales. "I've got one of you on my team to do that for me."

Number fifty-three: Aaron's new golden boy. Aaron gave him my old number on purpose. It was a reminder that he could always find a newer model to take my place.

"When was the last time you won a championship,

old man?" I swallowed the remnants of the pill dry. Its bitterness did wonders to kill the foul taste in the back of my mouth that I always got when I spoke to Aaron.

He glowered at me but ignored my question. We both knew it was the last full season I'd played that was worth a damn for him. Hell, he'd probably have won the season after that, too, if I hadn't broken contract the week before the big game.

It was the last championship he needed to win the most Super Bowls of any coach in history. The following year his rival surpassed him. I took that fame and glory from him by retiring the way I did.

If he were anything other than a monster, I might've even felt bad about it.

"You're selfish. That was always your biggest problem." Aaron pointed an accusing finger at me. "I listened to your big rah-rah speech in there. This is about every fan, blah blah blah. We can be heroes, blah blah blah."

Aaron made a jerking off gesture with his hand, which made my knuckles clench. My eyes narrowed as I ran through the ever-shrinking amount of reasons why I shouldn't bash his fucking teeth in.

"Where was all that 'brotherly pride' last time, when you abandoned your teammates, huh?" Aaron continued, walking a slow, wide circle around me. He was smart enough to stay well out of striking range. "A few of those fresh-out-of-college boys choked so hard under the pressure, they washed out of the league after that season. One even offed himself. Rope and note. Naaaasty business. Where was your pep talk then, Reaper?"

John Jeffers. I read about it in the news the day after it happened. We weren't close, but I knew he looked up to me. John also suffered from depression. He didn't take any medication, for fear of popping hot on a drug test. Still... I could never shake feeling a little responsible for what happened to him. That was the most important day of his life, and I wasn't there.

"You talk one hell of a good game, but when push comes to shove, you're in it only for yourself."

"What I'm doing is bigger than me," I spat.

"Is that what you tell yourself?" Aaron laughed uproariously. "That's why you're out here nearly getting yourself killed? Another good sack and sweet little Jackie will be growing up without a daddy. You doing this for her? You can't bullshit a bullshitter, boy."

Aaron's chest was puffed up with the confidence of a tyrant when he walked up to me. He looked up and blew smoke in my face. My right hand snatched his collar on pure instinct.

"Don't kid yourself, Garrett." Aaron wheezed as I brought him up onto his tiptoes. "You're here because you need to know, just like I do. You're just like me. The only exception is that I'm honest about who I am."

A sharp crack against my back staggered me forward,

but my pads absorbed most of the blow. It was the bat to the outside of my left knee that brought me to the ground. After that, all I saw was the stomping of boots.

There were three of them. They wore the uniform and pads of players, but were probably reserve guys Aaron was training. It didn't surprise me that they were his personal bodyguards, too. Aaron had a cultish way of training his guys. He made it crystal clear that if they wanted money, fame, and a career in football, they had to do whatever he said.

I looked around for help, but everyone was already on the field warming up and stretching for the second half. The entrance tunnel was dark and empty. The pads helped a little when I was on the ground and the Vicodin hadn't kicked in yet.

I hadn't felt the full shattering pain of every blow, but it was still bad, and if this continued much longer, I wasn't walking away without something being broken.

"That's enough," Aaron Miller's now raspy voice said, and the beating stopped. He took a knee near my head. "I want you to know that this isn't about the game. I don't give a fuck about these people, or their stupid fucking town. I'll burn it all to the ground and piss on the ashes if it stands in my way. I'm going to crush you for what you took from me."

"Garrett!" Judy's voice echoed off the concrete tunnel's walls.

No… not her not now!

I tried to yell out to her to run, but I couldn't take in the air to scream. I didn't care what happened to me, but I couldn't lose her.

"What the hell is going on here?" another voice asked. I cocked my head and through the bloody gash above my eye, I could see Judy's father Paul step in front of her. "You get the hell off him!"

"Heya, Paul." Aaron nervously plucked off his cap and brushed his wispy hair to the side, before replacing it again. He did his best to smile but came off like an overzealous car salesman. His rage and pride distracted him from how much time had passed. Halftime wasn't that long; eventually someone would come looking for me. "Garrett just tripped. We were helping him back up, that's all."

"Bullshit!" Judy yelled. She tried to get around her father to help me, but thankfully, Paul held her back. Judy was more furious than I'd ever seen her. "We saw what you did!"

"I guess it'll be your word against mine then, little girl." Aaron dropped the friendly façade.

"Yeah. You, me, and everyone else who watches this video," Judy spat, holding up her phone. "Smile, asshole."

Clever girl. It was a good plan. I was impressed by

her quick thinking, but I still hated that she was here. It was too dangerous!

I grabbed Aaron's pant leg, stopping him from walking over to Judy and her father. Aaron's face turned red as he glared at me. He stomped on my hand, then kicked me across the face. I still wouldn't let go. "Get that phone." He scowled at his guys.

Two of the minor league guys sprinted to Judy and Paul. Judy ran to get help, but these guys were professional athletes. They were on her too quickly. She didn't stand a chance. One of them snatched the phone away and smashed it on the ground, stomping it over and over for good measure. Damn, so much for that.

Aaron's bodyguard that stayed behind pried my hand off his boss, then gave me a few extra kicks for good measure. Fortunately for me, the meds had finally kicked in so I barely felt them.

"You got your evidence, Aaron." I spat out a wad of blood and gore. Getting back up, my only priority was getting Judy and her father out of this safely. "Let them go."

"You have such a soft spot for your playthings, Garrett." Aaron pulled what looked like a garage door opener out of his pocket and closed the gate at the tunnel's exit, effectively blocking us off from the field. Red emergency lighting kicked on and gave the bare polished walls a hellish tint. "I remember when your wife died. You were such a pain in the ass about it. What would happen if I took Judy from you? I hear you two have become awfully close."

The minor league bodyguard abruptly pinned me to the concrete wall. I strained against him, but without the use of my other arm, I was screwed. He wasn't as big as Nate, but he was close. This guy would definitely be a linebacker.

"Don't you fucking dare!" I yelled, struggling against a wall of meat and getting smashed back into the concrete for my effort.

"Or what?" Aaron asked with genuine curiosity. "There are no cameras in here. I've got a top-notch staff of lawyers that have gotten me out of so much worse than this."

"Listen here, Mr. Miller." Paul puffed up his chest and repositioned himself in front of his daughter. "This is outrageous! When the board of—"

Aaron glanced at one of his guys, then cocked his head toward Paul. The guard clocked the poor man in the face, dropping him like a sack of potatoes. Judy gasped and fell to her knees trying to comfort her father.

Aaron hovered over both of them. He menacingly whistled "Hey Jude" by the Beatles, while considering his options.

Suddenly the locker door behind us opened and white light flooded the room.

"It's too dark. I told you this wasn't the right way."

"Lucas, we're looking for a giant tunnel. Of course this is the...." Richard King surveyed the scene. Both King Brothers were decked out in full pads and wore Reaper uniforms.

What the hell were they doing here?

"Who the fuck are you?" Aaron asked, slowly taking the cigar out of his mouth.

"Today, we're linebackers," Richard answered quickly. There was an edge to his voice. "Judy, are you all right?"

"No." The fright in her voice made my heart stutter. "That is the opposite of what I am right now."

"Whoever you are, you'd better start explaining yourself." Richard stalked forward, knuckles clenched. Richard King was taller, but Lucas had twenty pounds on him. Both of them looked like monsters in all those pads. Neither would have a problem being a proper linebacker.

I couldn't wait to see Nate's expression.

"Is this the prick that's fucking with our town?" Lucas called out. He took a few jogging steps and shoved the guard off me, knocking the big bastard on his ass.

"Yeah," I said, peeling myself off the wall. The painkillers were starting to take effect. It still sucked and I could feel everything that happened to me, but I didn't care as much. I'd be able to push through the pain at least until the end of the game. "Thanks."

Lucas gave me a look that said we weren't friends. We just had a common enemy at the moment. At some point we were going to have to discuss what happened in Berlin, but now wasn't the time.

Fine, whatever. I'd take any help I could get.

With Richard between Lucas and me, the three of us advanced on Aaron. The hostility that radiated from us was palpable. Three versus three. Despite it being an even match numbers-wise, with how angry we were, they might as well be facing an army.

"Yes well, we've got a game to finish." Not liking his odds, Aaron groped for the remote in his pocket and raised the gate. Aaron jerked his head and his body-guards followed him out toward the field.

Judy kicked her leg out catching Aaron's foot and sending the fat bastard tumbling. Aaron's body guards paused to double back for him, but we were already on him. Richard and Lucas kept the other players at bay while I hoisted Aaron up by the collar of his jacket.

"Think about what you're doing, Garrett."

I jerked his face up next to mine and snarled. "I've been thinking about this for a long, long time."

I was willing to let it go; I really was. I had my own life outside of football. I could get past it all, but he just couldn't help himself. I didn't know what he was going to do to Judy, but, whatever it was, he was going to make sure I watched.

I couldn't let that go.

I threw him face-first into the sidewall. He hit with a wet-sounding crack and came away bloody.

"Help me, you fucks!" he growled at his guys, red spittle sprayed from his mouth. Between Richard and Lucas, none of them could get through. Anyone who tried got put on their ass, or worse. For billionaires, the King brothers were tougher than you'd expect.

Aaron turned over and collapsed into a sitting position against the wall. I took a knee over him and batted away his meager defenses. It was time to end our rivalry once and for all. I cocked my fist back, ready to ram it down Aaron's throat when a gentle hand on my shoulder stopped me.

"Let him go," Paul said, nursing a puffy eye. Aside from what was going to be a nice shiner, Paul was fine. "Do you really want to go down that path?"

"You're goddamn right I want to." All I saw was red; the possibilities of what he would've done to Judy, had he not been stopped, darkened my head and heart like heavy rain clouds, crackling lightning.

"And then what?" Paul asked. "What happens to your daughter when you go to prison?"

I hesitated long enough for Jackie's face to flash in my mind.

"Fuck!" I punched the wall right next to Aaron's head. I knew Paul was right. I took a deep breath and stood up. "Get this trash out of my tunnel."

The three players grabbed their coach and hustled out onto the field.

"Are you fucking kidding me?" Judy asked anyone who would listen; her voice was thick with indignation. "I'm glad you didn't kill him, but that's our only other option? Just let him go? What? Are we just going to pretend like this didn't happen? That's insane!"

"He's still our financier." Paul looked away. He was extremely conflicted about all of this. At the end of the day, as far as he knew, Aaron was their only option to fund and save their town.

It didn't surprise me that Aaron kept such a big secret from the stadium chairman and the rest of the board members. For being as good a tactician as he was, Aaron wasn't a good businessman.

"I take it Aaron didn't tell you about our wager," I asked Paul.

"What wager? What are you talking about?" Confusion screwed up his features.

"Whoever wins this game wins the right to financially back the stadium."

"Why would you possibly want to help us now?" He looked even more confused somehow. "You already passed on us. Twice."

I took Judy's hand.

Richard grabbed his brother's shoulder to give us some space, but Lucas brushed it off. It was obvious that Lucas wanted to have a few more words with me before we hit the field.

"Don't be such a stubborn dick. They're having a moment," Richard said, throwing his brother in a head-lock, dragging him away. Luke pushed him off, but relented, and they bickered like only brothers could the whole way out of the tunnel.

"I love your daughter." I told Paul while looking at Judy. Judy squeezed my hand and smiled back at me. "I'm just as flawed and petty as anyone else, but Judy showed me a better path. She also showed me the beauty of your town, and all of its potential."

I wish I could say he jumped for joy and all that, but the truth was that things didn't work that way. He and I had an incredibly damaged relationship, and we had a long way to go for him to trust me.

Paul sighed, giving both of us a look separately. It was concern, but also begrudging consideration. It was a look that said, "If this was what you want, Judy, I'm willing to give it a shot."

"What happens if you do win?" he asked abruptly. Hard lines carved up his face. There was real worry in his features. "Are you going to fire me?"

"Do you like your job?" I gauged his face, reading his surprise. "Are you happy being in charge?"

"Happy? I don't—" Paul blustered. He'd probably never been asked that question before.

"The man I saw today refereeing was happy." I put my hand on his shoulder. "I'm not saying I'll make you a ref if you don't want to be, but if I win, things will change. That doesn't mean they have to be bad changes. You want what's best for your town. Well now, I want that, too. I'm invested. Hell, my daughter even loves it here. I promise I'll do right by you and everyone else who lives here."

"Even Lucas?" Judy slipped in a jab and a smirk.

"God help me, even Lucas." I looked past her to make sure Lucas was out of earshot, then winked at her. Turning back to Paul, I continued, "We'll find a good position for you, something that you enjoy and actually find fulfilling."

Paul contemplated everything for a short while. I didn't want this to be a deal with the devil for him. I wanted it to be a partnership of equals. And in the coming months, I'd need his expert knowledge of the area to make informed decisions.

That was, of course, if I won.

"All right," he said finally. He extended his hand with a resigned but understanding smile and shook mine. "Are you sure you're still up for this? You look like shit."

"Thanks." I shook my head at his honesty, then walked toward the tunnel exit. The field grew more expansive with each step I took towards it. Leaving the sport the way I did those many years ago, I always knew I had one game left in me. "Yeah, let's finish this."

THIRTY-TWO
JUDY

"What the shit!" Gloria mouthed the words angrily. Her ghostly, pale face turned a shade of red I'd never seen before. She'd covered her infant daughter's ears right before the outburst, just in case some of the swearing was loud enough to hear. She glowered through the glass of the warmed VIP box we were sitting in, and stared lasers into Aaron Miller on the sidelines. "And they let him finish the game!"

I explained what just happened and everything leading up to it, to both Gloria and Molly.

Gloria slowly bounced her blanketed newborn as Alisha slept fitfully in her arms. Gloria lowered her voice and continued, "If the men are too proud or too stupid, then we have to do something. He can't be allowed to get away with this." Gloria glanced back at Molly and me. "Can we call the cops?"

"Do we have any proof of what he wants to do to the town, or what he just did to Garrett and Paul?" Molly asked hopefully. "Anything at all that we could use?"

"I took a video, but they destroyed my phone before I could back it up to the Cloud." I crossed my arms and looked out onto the field.

The third quarter of the game was intense, and the final quarter was shaping up to be more of the same. I pleaded with Garrett not to play, especially after everything that just happened. I'd heard too many reports of athletes dropping dead from too many concussions; every hit he took scared the hell out of me.

Thank God for the King brothers. Now that they were covering Garrett, he didn't get tackled nearly as much. In fact, Garrett's team was able to catch up because they finally had the right amount of players.

Lucas was a lot stronger than the other team anticipated and was able to stop the heavier defensive guys, which in turn gave their quarterback several extra valuable seconds each play.

Surprisingly enough, it was Richard who had a natural affinity for the game. Gloria told me he played a little in college. It certainly showed. Richard was startlingly quick for a man as tall as he was. He slipped past the linebackers and got more sacks than any other player.

However, we were still behind by a few points and it was the last quarter. My stomach was in knots because of how much was riding on the next few plays. Aaron's wide receiver, number fifty-three, was disgustingly fast. Garrett came extremely close a few times, but just couldn't catch him. If fifty-three had the ball and a clear field in front of him, it was an all but guaranteed touchdown.

So far Garrett's team did everything they could to make sure that didn't happen, but part of me wondered if that was going to be enough. All it took was one mistake, and everything would come crashing down.

"Thank you." I smiled, turning back to the girls. "I really appreciate you and your spouses coming to help. This is all just so crazy. The fate of our town decided with a football game?" I laughed—not because it was funny, but because it was so ridiculous and terrifying.

I didn't even like football!

"This is our town, too." Molly put a hand on my shoulder.

"Yeah," Gloria added. "Even if we don't live here anymore. Caldwell Hope will always be home. The boys were excited to help."

"Even if Luke was a big baby about playing nice with Garrett." Molly shook her head.

"How did you get him to agree, Moll?" I knew how deep that rivalry went.

"I told him it wasn't about him and Garrett. It was bigger than all that. This was a fight to save the soul of our town." A creeping smirk raised the corner of Molly's lips. "I also told him if he won, we could try some butt stuff."

"No wonder he's kicking so much ass out there," Gloria said, laughing. Molly nodded, then we both laughed as well. It felt good to be around my friends again, especially during such a hard time.

"Hey, guys," Molly said, checking her phone. "I just got a text from a friend asking about the game."

"Okay? What about it?" I asked. Aaron Miller playing against Garrett Walker was probably going to make the news, in one way or another. I just didn't think it would happen so quickly.

The game wasn't publicly advertised, but it wasn't exactly a private event either; there were thousands of people here. I didn't think we even charged for admission. We just had the people who showed up sign liability waivers because of the construction.

"Judy, are you sure your phone was destroyed?" Molly asked distractedly. Gloria and I huddled around her as she pressed play on the video her friend sent her.

We heard Aaron's voice a second or two before I saw him. "...I don't give a fuck about these people or their stupid fucking town. I'll burn it all to the ground, and piss on the ashes, if it stands in my way." Garrett was on the ground after just taking a beating by Aaron's thugs. I had to look away. It was hard enough to live through once.

But how did this exist? I watched my phone get destroyed.

"Holy hell." Gloria's voice was distant and horrified while she watched, then when it was over, a smile spread across her lips. "You didn't record a video, Judy. You live-streamed it. There was nothing to destroy; it was getting uploaded as you filmed it!"

"It must've gone viral," Molly said. Her voice was tinged with disbelief. "Caldwell Hope needs to see this. They need to know what kind of man they're in bed with."

The crowd suddenly cheered uproariously, which drew my attention back onto the field. The board members were treating this game like a practice run, so the stadium lights flashed, a pop song blasted over the loud speakers, and the Jumbo Tron showed the replay. Lucas and Nate had made a hole for Garrett at the ten yard line, and he pushed through into the end zone. I looked at the score. We were ahead by three points.

Gears turned in my mind. What was the best way to get this video to everyone that mattered in town? The Jumbo Tron. "Bundle up, ladies. I have an idea!"

The three of us ran through the massive concourse that ringed the field. We passed all the food and beer stands, and all the memorabilia stores that were designed to separate fans from their money. Nothing was stocked yet; most of them didn't even have signs yet. It reminded me just how much work was left to finish this stadium.

The thought of Aaron Miller being the one to pay for it all sent a shiver through me.

It was incredibly important that we got to the control room before the game was over and the people left. And like most important things, it was on the opposite end of the stadium from where we were.

Because of course it was.

"Okay, we're here," I said in between long, deep breaths. Garrett would be ashamed at how winded I was. The elevator was locked to the public, but that was fine. I always carried my key card. I slid it in the slot and nothing happened. The doors refused to open. I tried it four more times just to be sure. "Oh no...."

"The elevators don't work, do they?" Gloria sighed, catching her breath. Even her infant daughter, Alisha, looked irritated by the turn of events.

"It's not so much that they don't work." I groaned "It's more like they aren't even installed yet. Shit!"

"Guys, we're running out of time." Molly, who was barely winded, looked out the nearby window. I followed her gaze. Just under five minutes on the play clock. "Is there another way up? How many stories is it?"

"Six," I replied, and we all whined in unison.

Everyone important to Caldwell Hope was in the

audience, including the mayor and governor. Most of our town's decision makers weren't internet savvy. By the time they saw the video on their own, who knows what kind of damage Aaron could've done? We needed everyone to see this now.

"Hold on, kiddo." Gloria adjusted Alisha in her baby harness. "Mommy and her friends are going to do something really stupid."

"Five minutes. Six stories." Molly took a deep breath. "Does everyone have their big girl pants on?"

"Nope," I replied, saying what we were all thinking. I pushed open the stairwell door and we all shared the same resigned, "do we have to" look.

What else could we do?

Despite the unheated stairwell in the heart of winter, we were all sweaty messes when we finally made it to the top. If it wasn't for Aaron calling a timeout at the beginning of the last minute, we'd never have made it.

The door was of course locked, because of the millions of dollars' worth of equipment inside so I had to reach for my key card. Only... my card wasn't there!

I frantically searched my pockets and they all turned up empty. It had to have fallen out of my pocket. I looked around the floor then opened the door to the stairwell, but nothing. It was nowhere to be found. My heart crashed into my stomach and I slid down a nearby wall, feeling nauseous. All the work for nothing.

"Oh for— To hell with this!" Gloria apologized to Alisha, then kissed her on the forehead. She then pounded on the control room door as loud as she could and screamed for them to open up.

It was no use. The room was notoriously loud and with so many people controlling so many things most of them wore headphones. No one would hear—

The door swung open.

"Hello?" Allen, the manager, asked. He was confused and a little annoyed at the racket, especially at such a crucial moment in the game. Gloria must have caught him the brief moment when he didn't have his headphones on. "Can I help you?"

I rocketed to my feet and explained the situation as quickly as I could. I snatched Molly's phone and waved it at him. "So yeah. We need you to plug this in or whatever."

"That's... not how any of this works. It's a one-hundred-thirty-foot long screen. I—I can't just plug someone's phone into it," Allen tried to explain.

We walked into the control room. There were five rows of workstations, each with their own instrument panel, sound board, and LCD screen. Beyond that, above the glass windows that looked down on the field itself, was a wall of screens that stretched up to the twenty-foot ceiling. Each screen on that wall had a grid of at least four live feeds from different angles.

Between all of the humming electronics and the thirty or so people talking, and buzzing from station to station, the room literally vibrated with activity. It was unlike anything I'd ever seen before.

"Listen, Allen." I refocused on what I was doing there. "This is extremely important, even more so than the actual game that's being played." I hated to have to go down this road, but.... "My father is your boss. This is footage of him being punched in the mouth by one of our financial backer's goons."

"If you don't play this right now..." Gloria took several menacing steps toward the tall IT manager. She was far too intimidating when she wanted to be, especially for being such a short woman. "...bad things are going to happen."

"Fuck, all right." Allen retreated a step, and bumped into the back of someone's chair. They were so zoned into what they were doing, they hardly even noticed.

"Language!" Gloria interrupted harshly, covering her daughter's ears.

I could've laughed at how much Gloria changed since having Alisha. The Gloria I knew could cuss like a biker. I was willing to bet she still did when her daughter wasn't around.

Frustrated and thoroughly outnumbered, Allen shook his head and went to work on his computer. He mumbled to himself the whole time, but did what we asked. He didn't need the phone, the video was already all over social media. All we could do now was wait.

I walked over to the windows and watched the last of the game. There were ten seconds on the clock and we were still up by three points. We had the ball, so all Garrett's team needed to do was run down the clock and we were golden.

Jesus, we might just win this.

There was a defensive blitz, and our linebackers were overwhelmed. The quarterback had to throw the ball away, but he didn't throw it far enough.

Oh crap....

The ball's flight played out in slow motion. Out of nowhere, fifty-three leapt up and intercepted it. The gasp by the crowd was almost loud enough to rattle the windows. When he landed, everyone paused for a split second as they tried to figure out what had happened. That was all the time fifty-three needed to make a break for it.

"No!" I pounded on the glass, which made the woman working next to me incredibly nervous. Her monitor had the close up of fifty-three's run. I quickly sidled up next to her, and watched the play that was going to ruin us.

My rib cage weighed a thousand pounds as I watched that smug bastard twist around one player and leap clear over another who went for his legs. No one could get hands on him. Soon there was nothing but open field between the fastest player in the NFL and the end zone that would win the game.

The buzzer rang indicating that the game was effectively over after this play was finished. I began to hang my head as fifty-three left everyone else in the dust. He devoured ten-yard markers like they were nothing at all. When he hit the thirty-yard line, the camera pulled back enough to see that one man was actually on his heels.

It was Garrett, our own number fifty-three!

"Go, go!" I yelled as loud as I could. I knew he couldn't hear me, but maybe somehow he could feel me pulling for him. Garrett looked ridiculous running that fast with one arm pinned to his chest, but he somehow made it work.

The twenty-yard marker blurred by, then the ten. For as fast as Garrett was, that young kid was just a little faster. Garrett wasn't going to catch him.

Dammit!

Garrett must've known that, too, because he dug deep and threw himself at the player with all his strength. It didn't matter that he had one arm and was beat to all-hell. Garrett had more heart than Aaron's whole team put together.

He caught fifty-three's ankle and held on for dear life. Both men hit the turf, like a car crash, and the ball slipped from fifty-three's hands and rolled into the end zone. Both men lay there exhausted for a second, while everyone that had previously given up the chase made a frenzied dash for the football.

"What does that mean?" I asked in a panic. "Did we lose? What's going on?"

"The ball is in the end zone. If the home team gets the ball, they score another touchdown. If the away team gets it, the game is over," the women next to me quickly explained, while masterfully working buttons and sliders on her console. "Basically, the first man to pick up the ball wins the game."

Garrett and fifty-three scrambled to their feet and lunged for the ball at the same time. Dad blew the whistle ending play and ran over to the two-man pile players. When the men rolled over it was Garrett, and not fifty-three, who had the ball.

Dad let one of the field judges make the final call. The man was put up on the big screen. "Number fifty-three, Garrett Walker, has the ball. Garrett's team wins."

The audience exploded. Most were happy, some were angry, but everyone was screaming.

You did it, Garrett. I was all smiles when I glanced back at Molly and Gloria. They were hugging and laughing. Then I saw Garrett's exhausted face on one of the screens. He was looking for me in the VIP boxes. *You kept your crazy promise.*

Allen looked up from his monitor, caught my eyes

and nodded. The Jumbo Tron switched from players celebrating to a much more intimate shot of the closed player's entrance tunnel. It took a few seconds for the audio to connect, but when it did, it was as loud as the rock song that it interrupted.

Aaron Miller was finally exposed. His threats were loud and clear. Boos and shouts from the crowd almost drowned out the video's audio. Immediately, the audience turned on him. One of the feeds in the control room showed Aaron retreating in a panic.

Go ahead and run, I thought. The people of Caldwell Hope would never trust him after watching that.

The thirty-second video played on loop half a dozen times before Allen killed the feed.

"You did it." Gloria hugged me. "I'm so proud of you!"

"It wasn't just me." I could feel the blushing coming on something fierce. All I wanted was to run down to Garrett and wrap my arms around him. We'd finally won.

"Hey, hey, hey...." Molly wore a huge grin as she groped for me without actually looking my way. "I think you'd better see this."

Garrett was on the big screen; he tore off his helmet and called for a microphone.

"Just over five years ago, I met a woman who was perfect for me." Garrett's voice echoed out over thousands of fans. "Unfortunately, neither of us was in the right place at the time.

"Years came and went, and this emptiness grew inside of me. I tried to fill it in the worst possible ways. It was like trying to ram a square peg into a round hole. I just got beat up, and in the end was left with nothing but bruises. If it wasn't for my daughter...." Garrett trailed off, letting the words linger on the freezing winter breeze.

"That was until I came back to Caldwell Hope as a potential investor for the stadium. I never gave your town a fair chance, and because of that, you had to reach out to monsters like Aaron Miller. For that, I'm sorry.

"It was only recently that someone opened my eyes to the hidden beauty, and the true potential, of what Caldwell Hope had to offer. She made me fall in love with this town, with all of you, and with her.

"I want to be your partner and help the stadium, and all of Caldwell Hope thrive. I also have another request." Garrett painfully lowered himself down on one knee.

Was he really doing this?

My stomach became a tornado of butterflies. I had to clamp both hands over my mouth to keep myself from squealing. The crowd had no such reservations—they lost their fucking minds.

"Judy Sullivan." Garrett had to wait until the

screams quieted down again. "Will you be the round peg to my heart's round hole? Will you marry me?"

Tears flowed down my face as I nodded and mouthed a word that he couldn't possibly see.

"Judy!" Gloria whisper yelled from over my shoulder. I brushed my tears away and looked at her. Gloria pointed at a camera that Allen was pointing at me. I glanced past the tall IT guy and looked out the window. I was on the Jumbo Tron now.

And I was a crybaby mess.

I wiped my face again, but it didn't help. I nodded and said yes, but there was no audio. There didn't need to be. The crowd started chanting. "SHE. SAID. YES. SHE. SAID. YES."

"You'd better get down there, Judy." Molly said, smiling with her soft eyes. "Your future husband is waiting."

It took me about ten minutes to get back down to the field. It turned out there was another elevator further down the hall, which made the return trip way easier. I saw Garrett thanking Nate and the rest of the players for everything when I stepped onto the field.

Lucas and Garrett even shook hands. I couldn't make out the words they said, because of the whipping wind and the residual post-game noise. The tone wasn't hostile, however. If anything, it was borderline respectful. They weren't fast friends by any means, but perhaps playing together on the same team for once helped heal some of the scars between them.

"You're crazy, you know that?" I laughed, burying myself in Garrett's great, warm embrace. The crowd had mostly disappeared, but the few hundred people that remained gave us big "AWWWs" when I ran up and kissed my fiancé.

"I'm a lot of things." Garrett kissed me again. "But what I want to be now, and for the rest of my life, is a husband and a father. Let's go home."

Three Weeks Later

"What do you think?" Garrett asked.

"What do you mean what do I think?" I was blown away. Truly. "How did you...?" I lost my train of thought as I walked around the hall and marveled at all the details. The paintings, the small abstract sculptures, everything was just as I remembered.

"I recreated as much as I could from the pictures I found. A few things were a little trickier than others, but all in all, I think it's pretty spot on." Garrett walked over to me with two glasses of wine.

"It's perfect!" I took a glass. "We don't have masks though."

He'd rented out the golf course clubhouse where we'd first met and recreated the masquerade ball, except that there were no other people. It was just us, the band, and the waitstaff. We had the whole building to ourselves.

"That's what screwed everything up in the first place." Garrett took a sip of his wine and winked. "Besides, we don't have anyone left to hide from."

It reminded me of that dream I had where we danced naked in the hall.

"May I?" He put down his glass and stretched out his gloved hand.

I smiled, nodded, and took his hand. Our heels clicked along the orange and black floor as he led me into the center of the hall. Garrett nodded to the band, and they started to play. It was slow and nice, and had a lot of violin, which I liked.

Garrett slid a hand around my back and led the dance. His arm had healed enough in these past few weeks that he could wear a thinner cast. He had to get shirts and suits custom made to fit the cast; most of the time you couldn't even tell he'd fractured it in two places.

The midnight-blue evening gown with a star pattern printed all over it he'd gotten me still fit perfectly despite the faint baby bump. So much had happened since he'd mailed it to me that I never actually thought I'd wear it.

I chuckled, remembering I had thought it was a bomb from my student loan providers.

"How does Jackie like her new school?" I asked.

Garrett bought us a house within an easy drive of Matt Baker Elementary School. Jackie was doing much better. There were a lot fewer temper tantrums and outbursts. I thought it had something to do with both of us being around for her all the time now. I didn't think she felt like we were going anywhere on her, and because of that, she was able to relax a little more.

I could never replace her real mother, but we bonded pretty tightly and that's not something I would ever give up. I loved Jackie and thought of her as my daughter, just as much as the baby I was carrying.

"She loves it." There was a look of relief on Garrett's face. That was his biggest worry about moving to Caldwell Hope. "Molly says she's still a handful. Then again Molly says all kids that age are, so I'm not too worried. I'm just glad that Jackie is at least making a few friends."

"Hey, before I forget." I tapped Garrett's chest excitedly. "Dad wants to have us over this weekend. He says he has a present for you."

Ever since Garrett proposed to me, Dad has taken a real liking to him. That was almost more surprising than Garrett and Lucas burying the hatchet. They talked about football, and bounced public works ideas off each other. I think Garrett was Dad's new William King.

Garrett decided early on to change the theme of the stadium, from a twisted homage to him, to something that represented the town better. It was now the home of the Caldwell Hope Kings football teams.

The Grim Reaper was finally dead, and Garrett was much happier for it.

"Sure," he said. "If it's my college ball, I promise not to turn him down again."

"You'd better not!"

Garrett smirked and dipped me. When he brought me back up, he planted a kiss on my lips, then my nose, chin, and the side of my neck. I silently gasped in air. I loved that he could still make me feel those butterflies.

"You hear about the limo driver?" Garrett asked.

"Did he come out of his coma?"

"Yes. He even somehow remembered the license plate of the car that hit us. It'll take some time for the police to backtrack, but at least they have a starting point."

We both knew that it would eventually end with Aaron Miller, but Garrett didn't want to think about that little man anymore so I didn't bring it up. Instead, I decided to change the subject.

"What do you hope the baby is?"

"I want a boy," Garrett replied instantly.

"So you can teach him football or business?"

"He can do whatever the hell he wants." Garrett laughed. "But I hope he becomes an artist like his mother."

I laughed and kissed him on the cheek.

"I hope you don't mind, but I got you something."

I regarded him carefully. Something from Garrett Walker could be a card or a private cruise ship. "It's your birthday. I'm the one who should be getting you things."

"There's a modest space downtown next to Black Rocket Records that's been empty for a few years, I'm told. I'd like to turn it into an art gallery." Garrett fished in his pocket and produced a small brass key. It looked a lot like the one I used to have for the Rocket.

"Is that so?" I flashed him a toothy grin. I quickly saw where this was going. It was a very sweet gesture, but thoughts of managing the Rocket began to plague me. "I appreciate the thought. I really do! I don't know if I want to own another small business. I'm really not cut out for all the paperwork, and long nights of tedious accounting. I just don't think I have it in me."

"Own?" He scoffed. "I'm going to run it. I just need you to fill it for me."

"So you just want me to paint?"

"I want you to do whatever you want. If it's an art gallery, great. If not, we'll come up with something else. I'm taking a big step back from work. I've worked enough for several lifetimes. Now I just want to take care of my kids. And my wife-to-be."

"A stay-at-home dad, huh? I like the sound of that."

Garrett didn't reply, but I thought he liked the sound

of that, too. We spent the rest of the night dancing and talking. The more I got to know him, the luckier I felt. We were different in so many ways, but I was certain that was one of the things that made us being together so special.

Finally the clock struck midnight. It was officially his birthday.

It wasn't a perfect life. He didn't make his financial goal, and there would be a lot of legal stuff in the future over what Aaron Miller tried to do. Then there was finishing the heavily in debt stadium and making that profitable.

All those problems felt so manageable now that we were together. We could help each other, and really bring the town together. This was a new chapter in the book of Caldwell Hope. It was a brighter day, and a brighter future.

"Happy birthday, Garrett," I said, wrapping my arms around him and squeezing him tightly. "I'm sorry you didn't hit your goal of thirty billion by thirty."

"I realize now that it was just another distraction." He hugged me, careful not to hurt any of his still healing ribs. "It wouldn't have made me happy."

"Are you happy now?" I looked up at him.

His azure blue eyes burned into me. "More than I'd ever thought possible."

Jackson Kane is a professional stuntman, athlete, romance author, and above all else, a hopeless romantic. From American Ninja Warrior, to some of your favorite films, Jackson brings a unique writing style forged from countless harrowing adventures.

He's a lover of travel, his fans, his romance author peers, dulce de leche, and all things beautifully weird and interesting. He invites you to relax, have a whiskey sour, and let him thrill and excite you in a way no other author can.

Jackson will show you what the world locks like through the eyes of a genuine *Bad Boy*. Come with him, and read dangerously.

ABOUT THE PUBLISHER

Hot Tree Publishing opened its doors in 2015 with an aspiration to bring quality fiction to the world of readers. With the initial focus on romance and a wide spread of romance subgenres, Hot Tree Publishing has since opened their first imprint, Tangled Tree Publishing, specializing in crime, mystery, suspense, and thriller.

Firmly seated in the industry as a leading editing provider to independent authors and small publishing houses, Hot Tree Publishing is the sister company to Hot Tree Editing, founded in 2012. Having established in-house editing and promotions, plus having a well-respected market presence, Hot Tree Publishing endeavors to be a leader in bringing quality stories to the world of readers.

Interested in discovering more amazing reads brought to you by Hot Tree Publishing? Head over to the website for information:

www.hottreepublishing.com